"In *So Lucky*, Nicola Griffith replicates the actual experience of becoming disabled. This genre-violating story begins straightforwardly, then slides into a hallucinatory exploration of the body, reality, and identity. It is disorienting, destabilizing, and game-changing. I have never read anything like it."

—RIVA LEHRER, artist and curator

"In Nicola Griffith's *So Lucky*, Mara is a vibrant, active, social justice–minded woman stalked by a phantom. The phantom threatens her work, her relationships—nothing less than her identity. This angry, funny, cleverly written novel about the onset of disability in a world that values fitness above all ushers in a new wave of disability stories. Or let's hope so."

—SUSAN NUSSBAUM, author of *Good Kings Bad Kings*

"Nicola Griffith's *So Lucky* is compelling reading, a tour de force of the onset of disability. This is the first novel I have read that describes an autobiographical experience of disability from Day One with a relentlessness that can parallel a disability itself. It is intense, sad, and dramatic, combining mystery, romance, terror (internal and external), and hope. Just like life itself."

—STEVEN E. BROWN, cofounder of the
Institute on Disability Culture

"Nicola Griffith's depiction of Mara, newly diagnosed with multiple sclerosis, shows how we, as humans, deal with anger and love, hopelessness and hope. Griffith's lean, taut prose, and her willingness to delve deeply into Mara's fears, transforms *So Lucky* into a story about what we all share: an unpredictable life filled with vulnerability and a need for community."

—KENNY FRIES, author of *In the Province of the Gods*

© JENNIFER DURHAM

NICOLA GRIFFITH

So Lucky

Nicola Griffith is a onetime self-defense instructor who turned to writing full-time upon being diagnosed with multiple sclerosis. She now holds a Ph.D. and is the multiple-award-winning author of seven novels—most recently *Hild* and the *Aud Torvingen* series—and a memoir. A native of Yorkshire, England, she lives with her wife, the writer Kelley Eskridge, in Seattle.

ALSO BY NICOLA GRIFFITH

FICTION

Hild
Ammonite
Slow River
The Blue Place
Stay
Always

NONFICTION

*And Now We Are Going to Have a Party: Liner Notes
to a Writer's Early Life*

SO LUCKY

SO LUCKY

NICOLA GRIFFITH

MCD X FSG ORIGINALS   FARRAR, STRAUS AND GIROUX   NEW YORK

MCD × FSG Originals
Farrar, Straus and Giroux
175 Varick Street, New York 10014

Library of Congress Cataloging-in-Publication Data
Names: Griffith, Nicola, author.
Title: So lucky / Nicola Griffith.
Description: First edition. | New York : MCD / FSG Originals, 2018.
Identifiers: LCCN 2017047906 | ISBN 9780374265922 (softcover)
Subjects: LCSH: Health services accessibility—United States—
    Fiction. | Multiple sclerosis—Psychological aspects—Fiction. |
    Life change events—Fiction. | GSAFD: Autobiographical fiction.
Classification: LCC PS3557.R48935 S67 2018 | DDC 813/.54—dc23
LC record available at https://lccn.loc.gov/2017047906

Designed by Abby Kagan

Our books may be purchased in bulk for promotional, educational,
or business use. Please contact your local bookseller or the Macmillan
Corporate and Premium Sales Department at 1-800-221-7945, extension
5442, or by e-mail at MacmillanSpecialMarkets@macmillan.com.

www.fsgoriginals.com • www.fsgbooks.com
Follow us on Twitter, Facebook, and Instagram at @fsgoriginals

10 9 8 7 6 5 4 3 2 1

For Kelley, partner in all things

SO LUCKY

It came for me in November, that loveliest of months in Atlanta: blue sky stinging with lemon sun, and squirrels screaming at each other over the pecans because they weren't fooled; they knew winter was coming. While Rose stood by her Subaru, irresolute, a large red-brown dogwood leaf—the same color as her hair—fell on its roof. She hated the mess of leaf fall, had threatened over the years to "cut that damned tree down." Too late now.

"Mara?" she said. "Are you sure it's all right?"

After fourteen years of course it wasn't all right, but, "Yes," I said, because she would leave anyway.

The shadows under her eyes, the tiny tight lines by her mouth, nearly broke my heart. I hoped the lover whose name I knew perfectly well but refused to use would know what to do when those lines crinkled down like concertinas, as they were doing now.

"You should get going," I said, before she could cry. "Traffic."

She shook her head, slow and baffled: *How did we get to this?*

I turned away. And tripped. *A slippery leaf,* I thought, if I thought anything at all. *A twig. Or that uneven bit of concrete we really should fix.* But it wasn't *we* anymore. It was just me.

AIYANA SAT, AS SHE ALWAYS DID, with her feet tucked under her and her close-cropped head dark against the far end of the sofa. I sat catty-corner in the armchair. The physical distance between us was a habit developed four years ago when, one summer evening in a bar after a softball game, sexual awareness unfurled between us. We never spoke of it but we knew that to come within the orbit of each other's skin-scent and cellular hum could end only one way: falling helplessly, spectacularly into the other's gravity well, momentarily brilliant like all falling stars, but doomed, because I loved Rose. And this friendship was too precious to burn.

The day had been warm enough for the end of summer, but the sun still set at November times. At twilight I opened the windows and cool air began to move through the house. The dark was not close and scented with humidity, not sappy with bright greens and hot pinks, but spare and smelling as brittle as the straw-colored winter lawn.

Aiyana turned her glass of Pinot, playing with the refraction of the floor lamp's low light. "So. She really left."

"She really did."

Her eyes were velvety but she said nothing because she was leaving, too. Two days before Rose asked for a divorce, Aiyana won funding for postdoc research at the University of Auckland's Douglas Human Brain Bank.

"You've booked your flight?"

She closed her eyes slowly, the way she said yes when not trusting herself to speak.

"When do you leave?"

"Two and a half weeks."

Two and a half weeks. No Rose, no Aiyana. "I need more wine."

In the kitchen I reached for the second bottle of Pinot already on the counter but then thought, *Fuck it*, and opened the wine fridge for the Barolo. My hand tingled and I shook it. Static maybe.

When I brought through the wine with fresh glasses she raised her eyebrows.

"If not now, then when?" I had been saving it for a fifteenth anniversary that would never come. I knelt by the coffee table. The cork made a satisfying *thock*, like the sound of summer tennis. I poured; it smelled of sun-baked dirt. I handed her a glass.

Perhaps because Rose was gone, or Aiyana was leaving, too, which made it safe, or maybe it was the smell of the wine or just that we wanted it that way, our finger-tips touched and my belly dropped, and now the music seemed to deepen and the air thicken to cream. Her nostrils flared. We were caught.

Her feet were the color of polished maple, perfect, not like mine, not hard from years of karate. They needed to be touched. I needed to touch them. She sat still, wine-glass in her hand, while I bent and brushed the side of one foot with one cheek, then the other. Under the soft, soft skin, tendon and bone flexed like steel hawsers as her toes curled and uncurled. I stroked the foot. I wanted to kiss it.

Her eyes were almost wholly black, fringed with dark-brown pleats. I kept stroking. She closed them slowly. I took the wineglass from her hand and put it on the table.

Our breath was fast, harsh, mutual. My cheek where it had touched her felt more alive than the rest of me and all I could think was how it would feel to lay my whole length against hers. So I did.

JOSH NEXT DOOR had forgotten to turn off his porch light again and through my bedroom window a slice of light curved over Aiyana's forehead, cheek, and chin. A face familiar from sweaty afternoons playing softball, drink-ing beer afterward, and sometimes coffee at the Flying

Biscuit. But strange here. Nothing like the face I was used to seeing on that pillow.

"What?"

She didn't smell like Rose, either. I slid an arm over her belly, breathed her in, then drew back and began to stroke in lazy circles. "Are you still going to Greensboro first?" Her grandmother lived there. Nana was old enough to be her great-grandmother, and to a woman of that generation, a granddaughter leaving for New Zealand was goodbye, a one-way trip.

"I can't think when you do that."

"Are you?"

"In ten days."

I dipped my finger into her belly button, in and out. "Will you come back?"

"It's just Greensboro, babe."

I butted her arm. "From New Zealand." The fellowship was for one year, extensible to two on mutual approval.

She arched so that her belly pushed into my hand and her head moved deeper into the pillow, and shadow. "Give me some incentive."

ROSE AND I HAD FALLEN INTO BED, fallen in love, fallen into a life together with no pause for assessment, no hesitation.

This was different. Aiyana and I already had a years-long friendship, an established relationship as separate individuals, not partners. The next week was full of missteps and surprises. We would stop, confused, in the middle of conversations, when I treated her as a partner of fourteen years or she treated me as a friend. I called her Rose, once, in bed; and on Saturday, when I suggested a special meal for two—one I'd already shopped for—it turned out she had plans for the afternoon and evening she hadn't thought to tell me about. Our schedules did not help: twelve-hour days for me at work—it was budget season—and Aiyana packing and wrapping up her life to move to the other side of the world. We talked briefly about trying to reschedule one or both of her flights so she had more than twenty-four hours in Atlanta when she got back from Greensboro, but her grandmother did not like her plans upset, and the Air New Zealand change fees were obscene.

Her flight to Greensboro was on a Monday, mid-morning, so I couldn't drive her to the airport. We said goodbye the night before; at work the next day two people remarked that I seemed to be in a good mood. Perhaps I was relieved to be on my own for a while; I wondered if she was, too, and immediately started missing her.

She had been in Greensboro two days when I got up from the too-big bed, sleepless, and went into the kitchen to make cocoa. I didn't turn on the lights. The white tile was shadowy under my bare feet, and hard against the calluses formed by kicking boards and punchbags. I opened the fridge, pulled out the milk, pushed the door closed, remembered I needed the cream too, and pivoted. A movement made a hundred times before, a thousand, ten thousand, except this time, instead of muscle and nerve performing their everyday miracle of coordination, I tilted to my right and started to fall. I tried to compensate, putting out my right leg, only it didn't move, and I kept going down, and now my temple was grazing the handle of the fridge, and the milk was flying out of my hand, and I was lying in the dark, half on my back, half on my side, naked and wet, and thinking, *What? What?*

THE NEUROLOGIST SAID: "IT'S MULTIPLE SCLEROSIS."

Multiple sclerosis. *Crippler of young adults*, the actor says, looking earnestly into the camera. *Give generously. Help us fight this terrible disease.* Multiple sclerosis.

"There's a lot we can do these—"

I shook my head. She stopped. I could imagine how I might look: the eyes-like-burnt-holes-in-a-paper-bag shock I had seen every day when I first became an HIV and AIDS counselor. *From now on you are different.* Diagnosis as death sentence. Doctor as priest. She stood next to me, holding out a paper cup of water. I sipped obediently, stared at the name embroidered in red on her white coat, *Marie Liang, PhD, MD*. I blinked, tried to make myself concentrate. "The tests are conclusive?"

She turned the screen so I could see the MRI images. Pointed to pictures of my spine. "Three lesions on the spine, here, here, and here. This one is very large." She clicked through to pictures of my brain. I could see my eyeballs, like boiled eggs. "A possible plaque on the left parietal lobe."

"Parietal lobe." I felt slow and stupid.

"The left parietal is responsible for speech, words. And your balance and coordination. Your optic nerve is fine. And your hearing." She sounded brisk, but very far away. "It is likely that you have relapsing-remitting MS. Exacerbated by stress."

She looked at me, waiting for questions, comments. Stress. My wife had left me. I had a hard job, always harder at this time of year, putting the budget together. "When will I get better? What about work?"

She glanced discreetly at my notes.

"I'm the executive director at Wynde House. GAP." I could not tell if she recognized the name or not. "The Georgia AIDS Partnership."

She kept looking at her notes, evidently found the relevant line, under *Employment*. Now that I had lesions on the brain, was I an unreliable source? "Fatigue may be a problem," she said. "Particularly during exacerbations. Do try to rest for the next few days."

We were at the height of our budget cycle. There was no *rest*. I hadn't even been to the dojo for three weeks. "What about exercise?"

"Some people find yoga helpful. I believe the MS Society runs a class."

Yoga. Chanting and crystals and goodwill to all men. I'd rather hit things.

"Read the literature I gave you. Next week we'll talk about therapies."

THE SUN WAS BRIGHT, but glittery now rather than hot, and most of the riders on the MARTA train wore light sweaters. Two tourists were in T-shirts. I downloaded a cheap book on MS. *Average lifespan following diagnosis of the disease is thirty years.* But *Average lifespan of sufferers can be up to 85 percent of normal.* Weasel words. I knew mortality figures, could slice them a hundred ways from Sunday, and if normal for all women was 78.9 and, as I'd just read, average age at diagnosis was 34, the difference between 85 percent of normal and 34 plus 30 was more than three years. So which was it? I looked at the front matter; it was an old book. *Percentage of victims still working two years after diagnosis: 80.* But *Percentage still working after five years: 45.* I looked it up: that hadn't changed.

I should call Aiyana, she was the one who knew about brains. But *Sufferer. Victim.* That was not what I wanted her to see when she looked at me.

THE EIGHT STONE STEPS leading to the front door of Wynde House looked steeper than usual. We had talked, over the years, of bringing the ramp from the back to the front but it had always slipped on the budget priorities. I gritted my teeth and hauled myself up the steps.

Christopher was there to take my coat as soon as I got in. "The booking manager at the Piedmont called. Some problem about the gala reception. I said you would call him today. Number's on your desk. I've added a meeting for tomorrow. The third quote came in for a data security audit. You won't like the numbers any better than the first two—"

Right now I seriously did not care about the safety of clients' personal information.

"—Max Washington, the mayor's new liaison, wants the afternoon meeting at one-thirty instead of two; and if you *can* manage the earlier time, I could squeeze in that Hate Crimes Task Force appointment with Captain Hernandez you had to cancel Tuesday, and still make the Primary Carers thing this afternoon . . ."

The heating system had switched to its winter setting and it was too hot. *Should the core temperature of the MS sufferer rise by more than one degree there will be danger of symptom exacerbation.*

I headed for my office. Strange prickles and pins and needles fizzed down the nerves of both legs. The carpet felt like thick mud. Christopher followed me.

"So, how did it go?"

He knew I had a medical appointment, that's all. I sat down cautiously. Conflicting messages boiled up my spine. "Tell you later." I was shocked at how tired I sounded. "I'd like you to cancel the meeting with Max. Put Hernandez off. And shut the door on your way out. Please."

He opened his mouth then closed it again, shrugged, and went back to his desk. He'd worked with me a long time.

I'd first volunteered at AID Atlanta as a teenager, after my sister was diagnosed with HIV and hepatitis C, when my mother ran the place and it was one step up from a community organization. Now there were HIV hospices, seminars, research assistantships; counselors and halfway homes and medical assistance with in-home care; specialist partners like Project Open Hand to cook and bring meals to those living with AIDS, and

PALS—Paws Are Loving Support—that rescued kittens and puppies from the pound, paid for their vaccinations and neutering, and took the pets to the homes of people who were sick. My office walls were dense with plaques and photos—teen-volunteer me, with Elton John at the end of the AIDS Walk; my mother with the then–Democratic presidential nominee, the governor, and André 3000—certificates, letters from grateful PWAs and/or their surviving families: "Dear Ms. Tagarelli, We were so glad that you and your organization were there to help poor Jacob/Shanendra/Memo in their hour of need." The letters from surviving lovers were touching and brave; the ones from families, bewildered. This was the human face of what we did. Over the years, I had overseen the consolidation of local HIV organizations into the many-tentacled, professional nonprofit agency that had become GAP. The new budget I was about to send to the board was for $8.4 million. I had made that possible. Me.

I stared at the polished veneer of my desk. This job, those photos, were all I had right now. My wife had left me. My mother had moved back to London where I hadn't lived since I was a child. Aiyana was in North Carolina and would soon leave for the other side of the planet. *Victim. Sufferer.* Not incentives to come back. My job would not hold my hand or bring me tea on a bad day. Who would? What was this society for people with

MS. People with MS, *PWMS*. Useless. You couldn't fund-raise without a catchy acronym.

The phone buzzed. "Yes?"

"It's Max on line two," Christopher said. "In person. He's annoyed."

"You deal with it."

A beat of silence. "But you need his support on the hospice budget proposals—"

"Please, Christopher, just deal with it."

"Fine."

He sounded irritated. I couldn't blame him. *Mood swings, particularly depression, are not uncommon in sufferers of MS. Victims*—Sufferer. Victim. Was that who I was now?

The phone buzzed again. Eventually it stopped. The door opened. Christopher peered through. "Mara, are you all right?"

He waited a moment but I said nothing. He sighed. "It's Rose, on line two. She says your phone is off and she needs to talk to you about picking up some stuff she left at the house. Shall I tell her you're not here?"

"Yes." He sighed again, more theatrically this time, then turned to go. "Christopher." He turned back. "I'm sorry. It's just, I can't . . . I think I will go home. I'm so tired."

———

IT WAS STRANGE TO BE AT HOME in the middle of a weekday. I wandered around, shaking my right hand as though I could fling off the tingle, looking at the place with new eyes: single story, open plan, no steps. Not many modifications to make if I ended up in a wheelchair. But all the light switches were at the wrong height, and I wouldn't be able to reach the faucets at the corner sink in the kitchen.

The landline rang. Rose was the only human being who used it. If I insisted on keeping the damn thing for emergencies then we should at least get some use out of it, she said. I reached for the phone with my left hand.

"What's going on?" she said. "I called Wynde House and they said you weren't at work today, and Louise says you were seen at the Shepard Building." Where every neurologist in town rents offices.

"It's nothing," I said. Like a child: afraid of the monster under the bed, more afraid to name it in case it came out. "How are you? How's . . . Louise?"

"We're fine." Had she always been so impatient? "It's you I'm worried about. You've had tests?"

The counters were too far off the ground for someone in a wheelchair. And the cabinets meant I wouldn't be able to get my legs under them.

Me. Smiling up from a wheelchair.

"Mara?"

And then I couldn't breathe. I couldn't find enough oxygen in the air I was sucking into my lungs. The walls began to rotate. I dropped the phone and tried to run for the bathroom but, like a chicken that is too stupid to know it's dead, I fell. I vomited on the rug, so dizzy that I wasn't even sure if my vomit was falling *down*, if I was lying *down*, which were the walls and which the ceiling.

LIANG GLANCED AT MY CHART, then checked the IV dripping prednisolone into my left arm. Even looking at it made me feel as though someone were dabbling their hand through my stomach.

My sister died from a heroin overdose. I watched her, many times, take the used needle from a friend, laugh, and squirt the bloody remnants at the wall. Watched, and reminded her to clean the works, wipe her skin with alcohol. Watched her tie off her arm, jack up the vein, dimple then puncture it with the needle. I had nightmares about steel sliding into blue veins, bloody hieroglyphs on the walls.

"Looks bruised," Liang said.

She shone a light in my eyes, made me follow her fingers. "Your eyesight seems fine." She scraped the bottom of my left foot: the toes curled and a visceral memory of my belly on Aiyana's caught my breath. She scraped my right foot. The toes did not curl. "How does that leg feel?"

"Cold. Numb." The words were still difficult, but at least I could now speak, and swallow, and breathe. I tried not to look at the respirator and oxygen tubes dangling like gutted snakes by the bed.

She banged on my knees and ankles and wrists, made a note on my chart. "At the doses of corticosteroid we've got you on, you may have some difficulty sleeping. I can give you something for that."

"When do I get out?"

"You're rehydrating nicely. Your vertigo has passed and your vital functions are more or less normal. But I'm concerned about the possibility of a recurrence of respiratory difficulties. You'll need to be on the IV another two days—"

"I can have that done at home." Just talking about it made me feel queasy.

"—but I would prefer to keep an eye on you for another day or two here. To make sure you rest." Perhaps I imagined the emphasis. "And there are . . . arrangements you'll have to make. A wheelchair. Someone to do the shopping and cleaning."

Who? "For how long?"

"I don't know." She pushed her glasses up her nose. "You could be better in a week. You could get worse. Frankly, a setback of this severity is not typical with relapsing-remitting MS." She looked at her watch. "The sooner you get started on drug therapies the better. Read that literature I gave you."

I had already read it. Glossy sales brochures full of pictures of clean-cut, unstressed, middle-class people with white teeth posed with clean and shiny mobility aids, or standing on top of a mountain, or riding a bike. Scaremongering text that boiled down to, *Take this or you'll be a total cripple.* The medical equivalent of *Go to Mass or you'll burn in Hell.* Mostly injectable drugs— subQ, IM, IV—some oral. The published research looked suspiciously cherry-picked. Even so, there were lots of black-box warnings that said, essentially, *This could ruin your immune system, destroy your liver, and might not work. But if you don't take it, you will never climb a mountain again.* They reminded me of old tampon adverts my mother used to sing a song about: buy this and magically be able to ride a white horse bareback through a field, dive from a high board, or play competitive tennis. And the drugs were insanely expensive, starting around $5,000 a month—which was the annual deductible on the healthcare plan I had chosen for GAP, when I was still invulnerable and immortal, without a pre-existing condition.

Another slick pamphlet was from the American Multiple Sclerosis Society; they used the same model as one of the drug adverts, this time on a bike on top of a mountain. I followed their URL and found that their website, like all selling sites, was designed to get your contact info. I wasn't ready for that yet, wasn't ready to belong to the society of victims and sufferers.

At the bottom of the pile were sign-up sheets for yoga, and support groups for depression and mindfulness—as though talking about it would help with holes in your brain. I tossed them all in the recycling bin, then frowned, and fished them out again. I'd gone through them more carefully. All the groups were run by hospital counselors, not peers. Not a single one by people with MS for people with MS.

ROSE PUT THE BAG ON THE FLOOR and scooted the chair closer. "What did Aiyana say?"

I said nothing.

"You haven't told her? But she's your closest—" Her face seemed to thicken and swell, like a pan of milk coming to the boil. She sat back. "Well, that didn't take long." Her laugh was short and hard. "But who am I to judge? The pot calling the—" She closed her eyes briefly. "Sorry. Forget it. It's—never mind." She took a breath. "I'm glad for you. Really. But you should tell her."

"I will." When the time was right.

She pushed the oxygen paraphernalia away and lifted the bag from the floor. She pulled items from it, one by one, and set them on the side table.

"Salad. Because I know the pap they serve here might kill you, even if nothing else does. And some of that disgusting vegetarian chili you like. Beer, because as your grandmother used to say, a bit of what you fancy does you good. Some books. Ah, these aren't for you."

Her tarot cards, wrapped in purple silk. When we first moved in together she used to read her cards every week. I would never let her read them for me. *Pretty-colored cardboard*, I'd said. *I don't believe in that shit.* After a childhood of charismatic Catholicism, I was allergic to anything I could not touch or quantify.

"I picked them up from the house this morning." *The house.* "I didn't think you'd mind." She stuffed them back in her bag. "You didn't tell me Josh had planted more of those weird vine things. Ah, here we go. Decent tea bags. Clean pajamas. And three chocolate truffles." It was an eight-mile drive to get those truffles, and the deli where she got the chili was four miles in the other direction. She even had my favorite dressing for the salad.

I blinked hard. I couldn't reach the tissues with my arm skewered by the IV. I let the tears leak into my ears and the corners of my mouth.

MY HAND WAS FINE, and my right leg, though noticeably weaker than my left, recovered enough so that I didn't limp until I'd walked more than a hundred yards. But I was deathly tired, and the prednisolone made me restless.

Overnight, temperatures fell and the air turned hard.

Eventually I picked up the phone. My mother was easy: I called and left a message—she never picked up; sometimes she did not bother to check messages for days. And mothers were mothers; they had to love you. But every time I brought up Aiyana's number I saw her stern-faced icon—*When you fight to be taken seriously you don't smile in photos*—and could not make the call.

AT WYNDE HOUSE I REREAD THE SUMMARY email from the Budget Committee. A muscle under my left eye tightened. I rubbed at it, then messaged Anton, the board chair.

<Available for a quick call?>

He was. "What's up?"

"The response to the budget. Specifically line item 91, the ramp."

"A new ramp is not a budget priority at this time."

"It should be."

"The Executive Committee feels that sidewalk remediation would cost too much."

"I'll find a way to raise the money."

"We need our ED focused on strategic issues, not details."

The muscle under my eye twitched. I flexed my face hideously to make it stop. "People with disabilities are not details."

"The current ramp is ADA compliant."

"It's round the back. Like a service entrance. It sends the message that the disabled are second-class citizens."

"That's a little extreme."

"Separate but equal is extreme? Perhaps you should talk to our disabled constituents."

He sighed. "Do we have data, a survey?"

"We do." I'd found the numbers two hours ago. "Seventeen point four percent of our users self-identify as disabled." Less than the general population.

"I meant of our disabled customers' satisfaction."

"We have never thought to ask our disabled customers anything as a group." That would have to change. "Meanwhile, we do have a satisfaction survey of one. Me."

Silence. Densely populated. "Perhaps you'd better tell me."

In the corner, where the walls met the ceiling, a fly walked in circles.

"Mara?"

"I have MS." Sufferer. Victim.

"Multiple sclerosis?"

No, you prick, I'm the new owner of Microsoft. Another silence. He was probably mentally running through our conversation, checking he hadn't said anything actionable.

"You're sure?"

"The doctors are. Lesions in my spine and brain."

"Mara, I'm so sorry." And I could hear it in his voice already: I was now on the other side of the divide, no longer one of Us but one of Them. "Do you need time off? Anything we can do to help—"

"Anything except the ramp."

As soon as the words were out of my mouth I wanted to snatch them back. The way to persuade Anton was to encourage him to feel wise and magnanimous, not slam him up against his own bias.

"Perhaps we should pick up this conversation when you're feeling a little calmer."

"I am perfectly fucking calm."

"Yes, well. Tomorrow, Mara."

I flicked the phone off viciously. Calmer my ass. Then he pinged me again.

<Again, so sorry to hear your health news.>

"Asshole," I said to the screen.

A minute later, another message:

<ExCom meets tonight. Need revised budget by 6pm.>

Oh, he was not going to win that easily. "Christopher!" I needed a list of the Executive Committee's personal numbers.

He stuck his head through the door.

"Get me . . . What?"

"Your face. It's wet."

A tear dripped on my desk. I stared at it.

"I'll bring you tissues."

I touched my face. Definitely wet. I never cried. Except for the two months after my little sister died, when I'd find myself huddled and weeping with no warning. But this time no one had died.

I had forgotten to ask him for those numbers. Fuck it, I'd just hide the ask in other budget items. I pulled up the spreadsheet all my direct reports had already argued over, corrected, and signed off on and began moving things around, recalculating, relabeling line items, faster and faster, lungs working, arteries wide. Budget martial arts.

Christopher brought tea with the tissues and set both down without comment. I did not look up as he closed the door quietly on the way out. I was too busy stabbing at the keys and cursing the screen. *Fuck you.* Sum. *Fuck you.* Average. *And the horse you rode in on.* Total. My heart throbbed like the engine of a freighter battling a storm.

When the numbers said what I wanted them to say, I imported the web sheet into Excel for the digitally illiterate on the Executive Committee, which was most of them, attached it as a PDF, which they could all read, and hit *send*. Eat that. Compliant my *ass*.

After two minutes of deep breathing my heart began to slow. I picked up my tea. Then, beyond the closed door,

I heard "Shit." Christopher never cursed. A moment later he knocked on the door—he never knocked, either—and came in. He looked uncertain.

I put the cup down. He shut the door behind him. "Are you quitting?"

"Quitting?"

"I just read what you said."

"What I said?"

"Mara . . ." He came forward, gestured at my screen. "May I?"

I nodded. He turned it to face him, typed, brought up the spreadsheet I'd just sent, turned it back again. "It's the budget," I said. I had no idea what he was trying to get at.

He leaned over and highlighted two line items. Stood back.

Where it should have been labeled *Maintenance/ Improvements* and *Miscellaneous* it read FUCK YOU and AND THE HORSE YOU RODE IN ON.

AIYANA CALLED FROM THE AIRPORT: her return from Greensboro was early; she was just waiting for her car. I told her I wasn't feeling great—but nothing contagious, not to worry. She said she'd pick up something from the Flying Biscuit on the way. When she arrived, her hair glistened with rain and she smelled of herself, and travel, and soup and still-warm biscuits. "I nearly tripped and died on your weird-ass neighbor's rake."

She kissed me gently, like it was the first time. Like we were shy. Maybe we were.

She held out the bags. "I got soup. Chicken and pumpkin." Her favorite. "I didn't know what you like when you're sick so I got biscuits and gravy, comfort food."

We kissed again, slowly. Dread and desire was a horrible combination.

"You look tired." When I didn't say anything, she said, "How about I shower while you heat things?"

While the water hissed in the background I focused on laying the table, pouring the soup into a pan, putting the biscuits in the warming drawer. I could say it was just bad cramps. Napkins. Maybe migraine. Spoons on the napkins. I should cut some lime; she liked lime in spicy soup.

When she emerged from the shower in my robe her hair still glistened, but now she smelled of my shampoo, my body lotion, my deodorant. The way Rose had after a shower, only then it had been our shampoo, our . . . Too confusing.

While we ate she talked about Nana. "I've told her ten thousand times I'm coming back but she doesn't believe me."

I nodded and cut my biscuit open. Normally I would slather it with butter before it got cold and stuff the dripping biscuit in my mouth, but today I just let it steam gently to itself.

"Hold on." She got up, went to her travel bag and rummaged for a minute, then came back with a sun-faded gray velvet bag. The scent of biscuit, pumpkin, and lime was joined by dusty lavender. I imagined the bag sitting in a drawer with a sachet of dried herbs, untouched, for a generation. She untied the silk rope at the top, tipped a shiny object onto her palm, and held it out.

An old-fashioned ring engraved with vines and flowers. "A wedding ring?"

"It was her mother's. I think it's her way of reminding me I'm married to the family, no matter what."

"Her way of reminding you to come back."

She hefted it. "I don't think so. I'd say she gave it to me so that every day, walking around in a new life she can't even imagine, I can keep her in my thoughts."

Should I buy her a ring? Was that what she was trying to say?

She looked at her right hand, as though considering which finger would work, then slipped it back in the bag, retied the rope, and put it in her pocket. She nodded at my unbuttered biscuit and barely touched soup. "Not hungry?"

"Tired. It's been a hard day." She put her ringless hand on mine, then held it, stroking the wrist bone with her thumb, waiting.

I gave her an edited version of what happened at work: the argument with the board chair about the ramp's importance, the slipup with the spreadsheet, Christopher pointing it out. She did not interrupt. "And I couldn't even delete it. It was an actual attached file. But I was just so angry. The angriest I've been in a long time." She waited some more. "Because of what Anton, the board chair, said. About the ramp. I was angry because—because I'm sick."

Though she did not draw back I could feel her bracing against the news. Her mother had died of uterine cancer just months after we met.

"Not like your mom. It's not cancer. It's not anything that will kill me. Not soon." I took a breath, then said it clinically, as though talking about someone else. "I have multiple sclerosis. The relapsing-remitting kind. There are treatments. I should be fine for years."

It's a strange thing to feel a body you know change inside without moving, a kind of shrinking away, like the sides of a cooling cake.

"I'm guessing that's how Anton looked, too."

She frowned. "You *told* him?"

I stared at her. "Of course I told him. I've been out all my life. I'm not going back in, not about anything."

She shook her head.

"It'll be fine. They've already accepted my apology. I'm taking tomorrow and Friday off, and we'll get back to the budget on Monday. They need me." I was the best ED they had ever had. I had the connections they needed.

"So, the MS. How long have you known?"

"Since Wednesday."

She sat back. A whole week.

An explanation would take all night. "Come to bed."

She was beautiful, she was fine, but when we got naked in bed together I started to weep and could not stop. I wanted to say, *Don't leave me*, but, like Rose, she would go anyway. I would not ask. But I could not stop thinking it, and I kept weeping. And so we spent our last night together as chaste as when we first met.

ON FRIDAY, Anton knocked on my door. I saw immediately how it was but asked him in anyway because it would make no difference.

He sat down and put his leather folder on the table. "The board is concerned," he said. "We believe it's time to focus on your own health rather than helping others. You can't guarantee that this, this emotional *lability* will never happen again."

I should never have told him about the brain lesions.

"There are lives at stake here. Vulnerable people who rely on our help and protection. Are you up to the weight of that responsibility when your own health is fragile?"

All those lives relying on a failing body and a slippery brain full of holes. And it would only get worse.

He saw the answer on my face and opened his folder. "The board offers a commitment to pay sixty-five percent of your salary for six months, as gratitude for your service."

Service: a faithful hound ready to be euthanized.

"This is a draft agreement—"

"And if I don't agree?"

"The offer might not hold next month, as we have not yet ratified the budget."

My budget. But *Percentage still working after five years: 45.* There had to be a reason for that. And Georgia was an at-will employment state; they could fire me at any time, for any reason, or no reason at all. I could not afford to be fired.

"Add health insurance." There would be no COBRA. As a responsible ED I had held insurance costs down by keeping head count under the threshold—and opting for the high deductible. "Eighteen months."

"Six."

We settled on a year.

———

CHRISTOPHER WENT VERY STILL. "From when?"

"Immediately." I looked around the outer office. It already felt alien. "I spoke to Anton this morning."

"You should have told me. I could have helped."

I nodded. I should have. But Christopher had seen enough reactions to diagnoses that he knew there was sometimes no logic to our responses.

"Will you have input on the post?"

I thought about it. "Probably." Who knew the job better?

He tilted his head speculatively. "Who do you fancy?"

Good old Christopher. He had seen enough people down and dying to know that the best medicine sometimes was to ignore the details and get straight to what matters: influence.

I UNPACKED THE LAST FEW THINGS from the box and hung the pictures of still-dewy me, and Mum, and Elton John on the kitchen wall. I checked the time—1:40 p.m.—and texted Aiyana.

<Skype?>

There were eighteen hours and half a world between us. In her peach-painted kitchen it was almost eight on a summer morning, and seventy degrees: perfect weather for someone with MS. Sunshine lit the wall beside her, and behind her a window looked out, a long way down, over blue-green sea. She was wearing the ring.

Her flight was fine. Bumpy. She was in a university condo near the bay for two weeks until she found her own place. She had eaten "something called Weet-Bix" for breakfast. It all felt . . . strange.

Her words barely made sense. I knew I should respond in some way but all I wanted was to be wrapped inside her breath, her warmth, to feel her heart beat close to mine.

"So, how are you?"

"You were right. They fired me."

"Fuck." Her image froze momentarily, then jerked back to life. "When?"

"Yesterday."

Her face was still so long I thought her image had frozen again, but then she said, "Do you—?"

"I have—"

"—need me—"

Skype hated it when we both tried to speak at once. She gestured for me to go first.

"I have insurance for one year." Insurance until she got back. If she got back. "I don't need you to do anything. It's not an emergency." It was my life. Unemployed. Sufferer. Victim. "I'll be fine."

"You're sure?"

Maybe it was the bandwidth but her voice seemed half a tone higher than usual. She was relieved. Of course she was relieved. If I was fine she would not have to even think about offering to come back. And while we chatted—the strange smells, New Zealand TV—a little voice in my head whispered: *She won't come back. Who would want to come back to a sad cripple?* And eventually the poor connection made the conversation too disjointed to continue.

I PHONED CARPENTERS and decorators and electricians and set about installing grab bars in the bathroom and moving the light switches lower down the walls. I hadn't had to use a wheelchair this time, but I might next. And there would be a *next*.

Rose did not approve, of course. It was a cold afternoon but we took our cocoa out onto the porch to get away from the noise and mess of the alterations. "You're supposed to be resting." Her breath steamed in the glittery sunshine.

I stared at the froth coating the sides of my mug. "Doing nothing makes me tense."

"Resting isn't doing nothing. Try reading. Think about the things you want to do with your life now you're not tied to that punishing work schedule."

Everything I ever wanted to do with my life involved using my body. Not just martial arts. I wanted to kayak the Intracoastal Waterway for days. I wanted to fall out of a plane with a parachute on my back, feel the *snap* of it breaking open, the rush of air, the tumble and roll as I hit the ground. I wanted to run a marathon. *My MS running behind me, grinning.*

"Mara?"

I just shook my head. "So, are you and Louise packed?"

Rose shifted in her chair. "I've been meaning to talk to you about that. I thought maybe I should postpone."

"You've been looking forward to it."

"Then why don't you come with us? No, really. Think about it. Caribbean sunshine, fresh air, good food. You won't be in the way, if that's what you're—"

In the way. "No, I'll be tucked up neatly in my wheelchair with a blanket over my knees, smiling nicely at the passersby because that's what cripples are supposed to do: smile and be nice because we're so dependent on the kindness of strangers. Fuck you."

She blinked. "You should be so lucky."

It was one of those automatic call-and-responses from our marriage. But we had never used it on each other.

"I'm sorry," I said shortly.

"No, you're not, but I forgive you anyway." She drained her cup. "I'll call tomorrow before we go to the airport. And, Mara, if you need anything, just call. I'll come."

She slid into her Subaru in a way I might not be able to ever again, and I waved her goodbye, glad to see her go, wishing she would come back. She had known me since I was eighteen: Mara Tagarelli, third-dan Shuto Kai black belt, director of Wynde House, wizard with numbers, smart and sexy and witty. She knew I wasn't the thin, unsteady, and quick-to-tears woman who was afraid she would end up in a wheelchair and whose health insurance would run out in eleven months. A broken thing left behind.

Josh next door was digging in the disorderly organic plot that used to be his front lawn. Higgledy-piggledy jungle of crap, Rose had called his efforts. And that was when it was green. Now it was all dead-looking gray sticks and straw over red dirt. But I knew nothing about yardwork. The closest I ever came was sitting on the back deck with a beer after a workout at the dojo. Gardening was Rose's thing.

"Hey," I called.

"How's it going?" His eyes wandered over a tangle of cane frames that as far as I could see served no purpose, spade dangling from his hand as though he had forgotten it existed. He was probably stoned again. Once or twice a year he had people over and they banged drums and sang under the moon, but apart from his garden he kept his house in good shape. I've had worse neighbors.

I researched MS deep into the night. Behind the tidy paths of medical wisdom lurked a swamp of alternative treatments and belief systems ready to suck in the unwary.

Bee-sting therapy, based on some sketchy and desperate theory about histamines, in which you let yourself be stung over and over, and sometimes died. Liberation therapy, in which your jugular vein was scraped out and stented, and sometimes you died. Bone marrow stem cell transplant, in which your whole immune system was destroyed and regrown, ended up growing back crooked anyway, and sometimes you died. The most recent fad seemed to be some kind of starvation diet.

I stared at the brochures Liang had given me. Those drugs were all based on the same theory: that MS was a disease of the immune system. I'd listened to Aiyana rant enough about methodology to see that their arguments were as full of holes as an MSer's brain. All the study discussions were larded with words like "most probably" and "likely" and "seems to." The official drug information sheets on so-called disease-modifying drugs said, "Method of action: unknown" or "not entirely understood." Guesses. Just another belief system. Fear therapy, all of it. But *Go to Mass or go to Hell*. Immunomodulation was Pascal's Wager, only with something to lose.

REBIF CAME IN PREFILLED SYRINGES which slotted into an automatic injector. *The exact process by which Rebif works to reduce exacerbation is unknown.* I began with what was called a titration pack, which ramped the dose up slowly, three times a week over four weeks.

A nurse came to the house for injection training. We sat across the kitchen table from each other while she ran through basic hygiene and methodically laid out her tools on a laminated mat helpfully illustrated with a syringe, an alcohol wipe, a cotton swab. She flipped a spiral-bound notebook to a page showing the outline of a human body, back and front. After a moment I realized I was not looking at a diagram of the brachial artery, vulnerable to a slash, but at the layer of fat at the back of the arm; not at the femoral artery, but the padding over the quadriceps; not the renal artery, ripe for a deadly thrust, but the belly fat below and to either side of the navel: all sites for subcutaneous injection, marked in tasteful green rectangles. The belly and thighs were the easiest, she said. The buttocks and arms sometimes required help.

I should wash my hands now, she said. Where would I like the first injection to go?

To go. Always passive or middle voice when pain is involved.

I dried my hands, sat down again. Belly, I said. I had read it was the easiest.

She nodded. This first one would be saline, so I only had to worry about the feel of the injection itself. Once I knew how that was supposed to go, I would inject myself with a very low dose of Rebif, just 8.8 mg, unlikely to cause any difficulty. Perhaps I had a friend who would sit with me for that?

"Of course," I said. Something I learned early at self-defense: never let them see your weakness. Be part of the herd, just like the rest, because if you have a limp, or white spots, or are facing in the wrong direction, you stand out, you're visible, and the predators zero in. There were only three people in the world I would let see me so vulnerable: one in New Zealand, one in England, and one on a Caribbean cruise. I stared at the syringe as she talked, trying not to see my sister laughing, puncturing her vein. I had never understood her willingness to breach bodily integrity, the layer between us and the world that keeps us safe. I remembered a poem I had heard long ago, *Where would we be without skin? / All over the bloody place . . .*

I lifted my T-shirt, then realized I'd need both hands for the injection, and took it off. My skin pebbled until it looked like coarse concrete; I should have turned the heat up. When I tore open the alcohol wipe my stomach squeezed, but I wiped deliberately, thoroughly at the round of my belly, two inches below and to the right of the navel. My hand was steady as I pulled off the needle cap. The needle was short and very fine. I wasn't cold anymore and my skin looked smooth and soft and vulnerable.

"Don't forget, if you can't pinch two inches, use a forty-five-degree angle," she said.

I was braced. I had read the horror stories online about the pain, the injection site reactions. I took a long, slow breath, and as I breathed out I slid the needle in. There was no resistance; I could have been made of air. It did not hurt. I wiped at the injection site with a dry cotton ball.

There might be blood when I did it for real, she said. And some people found it helpful to use a cold compress afterward. I should always dispose of the sharps properly, in the container provided. Remember to get the Rebif out of the fridge an hour before the injection.

She turned the spiral-bound notebook, with its drug company logo, Serono, a subsidiary of Merck, on the top right of every page. This was for me to keep, she said. I should record the sites in this section, *here*, and any reactions in this one, *here*.

And be reminded that Daddy Serono was looking after me; and the pain was for my own good.

I DID IT FOR REAL THAT EVENING. It stung going into my thigh, and blood beaded at the tiny puncture. I wiped it away. It beaded again. I wiped it away firmly, and waited. Nothing. I wanted to share my triumph. Mid-afternoon in Auckland. I tried Aiyana on Skype but she did not pick up. Maybe I should go out, get a drink with the loud, dog-loving women I played softball with in summer. But all the received wisdom about Rebif was that it was best to wait and see how you reacted.

Two hours later, watching Netflix, I ached as though I'd had a hard karate class, and the injection site itched. I pulled down my pants. There was a small red welt on my quad, like a fleabite.

It wasn't so bad.

THREE DAYS LATER, after two injections, the fatigue seemed to melt away. I went back to the dojo for the first time since the budget crunch. Bonnie was there. Her beginners' class was running a little late. She rolled her eyes at me—she hated teaching those classes, but it paid the rent—nodded as I came onto the practice mat, and pointed at the wall clock, mouthing *Five*. I stretched, carefully at first, then with growing confidence. Maybe I was one of the subset of people for whom those drugs actually worked. Maybe I would beat this thing.

Five minutes later she dismissed the class and came over. I was doing leg extensions. She put one of her big hands on my left knee, took the foot with her other, and started pushing. "It's been a while."

"Budget season." Maybe Rebif would mean I'd get to say that again one day. Fuck Anton.

She nodded. And for twenty minutes we said nothing more except move this, give me that, too much, go a bit harder.

"Second form?"

I nodded and stood, balanced and sharp as a jewel, ready to dance the karate kata while Bonnie acted as my opponent. I took the open-ready pose, breathed out, and began the slow-motion sink to a squat that would turn into the explosive first move. *Make it feel like butter sliding down the hot steel of a coiled spring*, Bonnie had said when she first taught me. Down I went, and down, oiled and smooth, feeling the muscles in my calves and thighs, in my ankles and at the base of my toes, gathering. I started the inhalation. *And when your lungs are full it's like that spring covered in butter just slips loose and you FLY up and out with the ki-ai, the karate shout.* I leapt with forearms crossed to block Bonnie's downward blow, and it was as though my smooth buttered spring had rusted—it gave under the strain, just broke—and I faltered and jerked, and half blocked Bonnie's fist with my fingers.

My hands dropped to my sides and swung there. We looked at each other.

She walked around me twice, and stopped. "What's going on?"

And I didn't know how to tell her, how to open my mouth and say: I am sick and possessed by disease and this thief is stealing my life.

"It isn't me," I said. "It's multiple sclerosis."

Her body didn't move, but her face changed, I saw it, a shuttering and turning away, just before she laid a hand on my arm and said, "I'm sorry."

"It's just that one move," I said. "I can do the rest."

"Sure," she said, but her smile was mechanical, the kind she gave her students—the not-real people—and twice while we worked I saw her glance up at the time. My face felt as white and hard as the clock's.

AT HOME I TURNED THE HEAT UP and showered a second time to get the feel of Bonnie's hand off my arm. Asshole, I thought, as the hot water spilled down the muscles of my back. Asshole. I could still fight, and better than most. I could run that dojo better than Bonnie, too, and teach. I imagined the lessons I could teach her, and my patronizing smile as she failed, and the exercise turned into imagining a real class.

I turned and let the hot water stream down my back. I could. I could teach beginners, at least on good days. Or maybe self-defense. It didn't have to be as precise as martial arts. Not physically. I turned off the shower and dried myself thoroughly, one muscle group at a time. The welt on my thigh was almost gone.

I sat in the kitchen in my robe with a cup of green tea, watching the dust motes dance in the slanting winter sunshine, absorbing the color of the cut flowers on the table and the sparkle of the brass handles on the cupboards. When my tea was gone, I decided to take a nap; it was a good reset button, something I had learned to do during my first budget season. I turned down the heat, took off my clothes, and climbed into bed. The sheets were clean and stretched tight and felt good. I could. I could teach. A jay scolded in a harsh, metallic voice.

A park at night, smelling cold and empty. From the shadows a laugh, dry as paper. I back up against a tree, and I know it's waiting on the other side, but I can't move, my legs are stuck, I am stuck, like a fly who lingered too long on sap-sticky bark now turning to amber. Trapped.

I woke to rain clouds dense as black mold and muscles slow with cold. I struggled into my robe and closed the curtains. Who was I kidding? A child could flatten me on a bad day. And there would be bad days. MS always got worse.

I was fearless until I was twenty-two; until one night in a bar I was beaten by two men and I learned the story that most women already knew: that men beat women for no other reason than they could, because they were raised on the story that women are weak. *We* were taught we are weak. The message was beamed at all of us, from all sides, from TV and radio, plays and movies, novels and jokes, comics and social media: we are weak, we must rely on the kindness of strangers, call forth a man's better nature, placate the savage beast. That night in the bar I understood on a visceral level what I had only known as a statistic: that women's fear was a marketable commodity. Fear sells.

The understanding had filled the twenty-two-year-old me with rage. I turned that rage into a goad: learned to fight, to smash wood with my hands, to stretch my body, to toughen it, make it harder, stronger. Learned to not be afraid; to break their narrative. But Rose had been there to hold me, to put her warmth between me and the fear. Now there was no Rose. No one and nothing to breathe comfortingly under my hand while this thing stole my life.

GOSPA AT PALS—Paws Are Loving Support—said, "Yeah, we have some kittens, but they're for people with HIV. Try the county animal shelter."

"It's three days before Christmas. There won't be anything left. I need this."

"Oh. Right. I heard—I forgot. Look . . ."

On the softball field we were sometimes rivals, some-times teammates, always easy with each other. But now her voice took on that note I was already sick of hearing: melodious, compassionate, the voice you use for those worse off than you, those you want to be nice to and then never, ever have to think about again. As a fund-raiser I'd loved to hear that voice; it meant I could squeeze a huge donation out of the speaker because they desper-ately wanted to make the unpleasantness go away and get on with their healthy lives.

". . . so if you can wait a few days I'll see what—"

"Forget it," I said. I'd never play softball again, anyway.

The fifth pet store I called, in a suburban mall, had a litter. "Just in, ma'am."

"Any females?"

"Four female, six male."

By the time I got there, an hour later, there were five left, tiny things with ears like satellite dishes and little bright eyes. One was on its own in a cage at about eye height, curled up tight as a kitty ammonite. I bent to look. It lifted its head and looked straight through me. It had white whiskers and a pink nose, fur the smudged beige-and-cream-and-smoke of fudge ripple ice cream. "Why is this one on its own?"

"She fights."

———

I CALLED HER MIZ RIP, because she looked like fudge ripple and she ripped up everything that got in her way, including me. And she purred all the time, like a ripsaw. She was as big as my hand with teeth like needles. The pads of her paws were even pinker than her nose. She followed me everywhere, investigated everything, settled on my lap as though she had been born there. She weighed less than a baby bird. I was ridiculously happy to feel her tiny rib cage tremble under my palm as I stroked her. She slept. "That's right," I whispered to her as her paws kicked in a kitten dream, "I'll protect you."

I sat without moving for nearly two hours as it got dark outside. Maybe I would get a Christmas tree after all. Miz Rip would enjoy pulling all the ornaments off.

A shadow flitted through my peripheral vision. I turned. Nothing. Maybe a light flickering somewhere.

JOSH NEXT DOOR HAD A NEW GIRLFRIEND, Apple, who invited the neighbors over for drinks. I ached from the Rebif more than usual and it had been two days since I'd talked to another human. I went to take my mind off it.

"And what do you do?" Apple asked me over a glass of hot cider—organic of course, but so heavily spiced it could have been boiled sap. Josh snaked his arm around her waist and gave her a loose grin. Her dress was warm orange, a snugly fitted sueded material that made her breasts look like satsumas I could heft on my palm.

"Nonprofit work. Or used to." I took another gulp of the sticky stuff. "I was let go. For being sick."

Cancer, I could see her think. Cancer was what everyone thought. "That's awful. Isn't it, Josh?"

"Totally lame," he said.

"For being a cripple," I said.

"*Totally* lame," he said.

The air behind me stirred, like someone standing too close, but when I turned, teeth bared, there was no one there. I blinked, caught between fight and flight.

"—great yard," he was saying. "It could feed you: artichokes, tomatoes, squash, all kinds of squash, asparagus—"

I finally caught up with what he was suggesting. "I don't grow things."

"No," Apple said. "The earth does."

"Right." Josh nodded. "Georgia dirt. Best in the world. Like, toss a cup of fruit salad from your car window and six months later the road'll be jungle. Anyone can do it."

Even poor lame cripples.

SKYPE WAS TOO FRUSTRATING and, like texting, not always useful with the eighteen-hour time difference. Aiyana and I began to talk mostly by email. In the middle of the night with Rip on my lap I could write anything. My latest included a picture of Rip, and a question I had not been able to find an answer to—I no longer had my GAP access to Emory's library—on the coincidence of MS and HIV. I signed, as I always had, *Love*, the kind of *love* you'd use for a family member or a very close friend. We had never said *I love you*.

I woke up to an email from her: not very long, but bright and warm, with a selfie of her and her two postgrads wearing shorts and Santa hats in a bar.

> You'd like them. Also, here's a PDF of a paper I
> found. I don't know if I buy it. I'm not saying I *don't*
> buy it; it's interesting: MS as a metabolic problem.
> Happy Christmas, love xx.

CHRISTMAS. Me, a cat, and an academic article; a soon-to-be ex-wife in the middle of the Caribbean, and a question mark on the other side of the world.

When Rip was fast asleep, belly drum-tight with roast chicken, I poured myself a glass of wine and opened the article. It was heavy on biochemistry. I had to keep stopping to highlight terms and go look them up. The third time I lost my place in the file I padded through to the office and printed it out.

Paper was better for close engagement. I could under-line in different colors, scribble in the margin, add sticky notes, all while looking up terms on the tablet: "foam cells," "PPARs," "OxLDL." It began to make sense. It took what was known about MS, the research results that had been reviewed and replicated, and reassembled them into some-thing new, a jigsaw puzzle in which, for the first time, all the pieces fit. There were no odd bits left out, none ham-mered in with brute force. The resulting hypothesis seemed elegant, clean, and clear: MS was a problem of faulty lipid metabolism. It was a direct consequence of high-sugar, high-animal-fat diets. A sort of atherosclerosis of the central nervous rather than the arterial system. It ex-plained so many puzzling aspects of the disease, such as why MS cases were on the rise, why it developed more often in women than men, why vitamin D was a huge influence, and more. But I couldn't find any treatments associated with this hypothesis, or any trials.

Maybe Josh was right, I should eat more vegetables. Maybe I'd think about it in spring.

ANOTHER TWO-DAY COLD SNAP. Rip huddled on my lap and I dug out a thick sweater. Aiyana texted a photo of herself in shorts and bikini top eating tofurkey on a beach.

<Summer school starts in 10 days! xx>
Nothing about HIV and MS.

TWO WEEKS INTO THE NEW YEAR I went to see the neurologist again. Her office suite was faced in polished marble. My reflection walked toward me as light as a dancer.

Liang thumped and prodded and um-hmmed to herself.

"I'm worried about my eyes," I said.

"Blurring? Double vision?"

"More like catching sight of something, like a reflection or a shadow. There one minute, gone the next."

"Hmm." She made me stand up, look side to side, follow her finger, close my eyes and open them. Shone a light in my eyes and peered intently. Her breath was moist and sweet. I stared at her name again. Marie. "No nystagmus." She clicked the light off. "There was nothing on the MRI that might indicate a problem. And I'm not seeing anything. Would you like a referral to an ophthalmologist?" I shook my head. "Where are you with the Rebif?"

"I'll be at the full twenty-two milligrams in about a week."

"How do you feel?"

"Some tenderness. Some aches. I get very tired the day after."

"Most people adjust. But I can prescribe something for that, just in case." She began to key in the prescription.

I sat down. "The makers of Rebif are Serono. A subsidiary of Merck."

She nodded, hit *enter*.

"They make something called Serostim. People with HIV take it for wasting."

She folded her hands in her lap with the deliberate patience I had come to loathe.

"Which got me thinking, so I did a search. People with HIV don't seem to get MS. Why is that?"

A pause. "Research is ongoing."

Some people hated to say, *I don't know*. But there was something there, I just didn't know what. "How does Rebif work?"

"It's believed—"

"Belief is not data. The data don't convince me that the main problem is the immune system."

"We use evidence-based medicine."

"The evidence is crap."

She sighed. "Denial at this stage is common."

Denial?

"What have you been reading?"

"Are you familiar with the lipid hypothesis?"

"The Swank diet has been—"

"Not a diet. A hypothesis. That MS is a lipid metabolism disorder. OxLDL, PPARs, all that stuff." It had all seemed so clear when I was looking at the diagrams and following the text, but now I could not recall it, exactly. "I can send you a copy."

"Of course. I'd be happy to take a look." She was not really listening. She stood up. "Meanwhile, the modafinil should help with the fatigue. I'd be happy to discuss these, ah, lipid theories at a later date."

I opened my mouth to say, *Hypothesis, and just one*, but a flash of movement in the corner of the room slapped the words back down my throat. Liang nodded pleasantly and left. It took me a long time to get over the irrational fear that something lurked on the other side of the door, waiting for me, grinning.

AT WYNDE HOUSE one of the first things the newly diagnosed were told was: Find your people. No one knows how it feels to go through what you're going through more than those going through it, too. No one can offer better advice. There were plenty of online groups, ranging from old-fashioned LISTSERVs to Facebook to Snapchat, and print magazines sponsored by various nonprofit and commercial organizations. I found one print journal, *MonSter!*, run by people with MS for people with MS. The website seemed a bit out-of-date, but they did not accept money or advertising from the medical-pharmaceutical industry. I signed up for a six-issue subscription.

Words were good, but physical, in-person connection was better. The closest thing I could find to local peer support was a group run by the American Multiple Sclerosis Society that met weekly.

At the DeKalb Community Center, I walked along the blank, airless corridor more and more slowly until I was barely moving at all. There were black streaks here and there on the floor. I imagined the thick rubber tips of canes and walkers squeaking on the vinyl, twisted feet dragging along, the tires of scooters and powered wheelchairs scuffing the walls. The door was painted dark blue, a lovely color, like twilight, the time to rest, to lay down the burden and hand over management of your life to others. The handle was brushed steel, a big lever suitable for people in wheelchairs. There was a disc button to hit, too, to open the door automatically.

I stopped. I ran support groups, I didn't join them. This meeting was for cripples, not people like me. Laughter hissed behind me to the left. Adrenaline jetted into my long muscles and swelled my heart and lungs. I turned slowly. Nothing. I turned back. Nothing. But the feeling of being watched did not go away.

I breathed, breathed some more. *Face your fear.* I went in.

I don't much like dogs. So of course the first thing I saw was a plump pug, the kind that always bites, wearing a beautifully dyed yellow collar and wheezing at the feet of a woman with skin wrinkled as a ruined grape. Her chestnut wig was styled in a 1970s pageboy, her cane propped next to her against the only empty chair. She gave me an ornery, milky stare, then flicked her attention to just beyond my left shoulder. Insult or attempted intimidation, I wasn't sure. But the first rule of self-defense was, Don't do what they want. Break the narrative.

"Hi," I said to the group. "I'm Mara. Just diagnosed." To the ruin, "Would you like to move that cane or should I?"

She brought her gaze back to mine and her expression changed to something I could not name and did not like. She moved her cane. I wanted to snatch it from her and break her skull with it, but beating the matriarch to death was not a good way to introduce yourself to a group, so I just nodded, and settled in.

The hired counselor was talking to the small circle in a *Now remember we're all here for each other, it's a safe space* tone that at Wynde House would have had her jeered from the room. Six women, two men. The other women were in their forties and fifties, two in power chairs. One had her arm immobilized in the kind of forearm splint I'd seen often as a volunteer at the women's shelter. All were white except one with straightened hair. Every one of them had the look of an untroubled Christian. One man was young with gleaming jaw-length hair and multiple piercings, the other late fifties and wearing a sports jacket with leg braces visible under his dress socks and loafers. The pug waddled over and snuffed at his ankle, then at the chair leg. If it was my chair I'd be shifting it out of the way before the dog could cock its leg, but the man didn't seem to notice it. No one was paying it any attention.

The counselor introduced herself as Wendy and asked the group to each offer one pearl of advice to me, the newcomer. What did they wish they had known when they were first diagnosed?

One of the women in a power chair advised me to find a hobby I could do lying down, just in case. Another suggested I use a shopping cart at Kroger, even if I was buying just eggs, because carts were great to lean on without anyone guessing there was anything wrong. She looked at me sadly and added, "And you have to do everything yourself, be ready for that." The older man told me on no account to get handicapped plates for my car because it was like having a target tattooed on your forehead; no, get the placard you could take down and tuck out of sight when you didn't need it.

The pug stuck its nose in one woman's purse. She ignored it. They all ignored it.

I felt as though I were surrounded by aliens. During my training I'd sat in on a lot of groups. AA meetings were wry, with an attitude of *Don't apologize, just improve.* HIV meetings crackled with rage and zest. Breast cancer meetings were war zones, full of stirring martial metaphors followed by weeping implosions. This group felt like nothing but self-pity and learned helplessness. Their shoulders were hunched, their eyes evasive, as if they all expected to be treated like victims, as though they had abnegated responsibility for their lives.

The pug sniffed my shoe and began to drool like they do just before they bite. I eased my foot away. It growled.

The old woman's bright gaze fastened on mine. "So you see him?"

See him?

The conversation had moved on. The pierced man was saying, "—whole left side went cold from the armpit down. Now it's numb. The neuro won't say if the feeling will come back. Mostly it does, he said. For most people, most of the time. So I'd just have to wait. But, *fuck*!" The woman in the sling flinched. "It's been weeks! I'm stressing *out*. How do you cope, waking up every day not knowing? And not knowing when it could happen again?" His voice trembled.

They all talked at once:

You can never know, only God knows—

—long had it been? Just five weeks? Well—

The old woman lifted her chin at me. "I'm the oldest person in the world with MS," she said, as though we were the only people in the room. But she was loud, like many people who were losing their hearing. The counselor flicked me an *Ignore her and she'll stop* look. The old woman caught it and stretched her mouth in a hideous grin. Her false teeth were dull and the fake gums a bubblegum pink, shocking next to the brown-splotched yellow of her skin. "Most folks die right around pension time. Just give up, lay down, and die. Not me. I'm ninety-one. I know some things. So you listen to me."

The rest of the group talked on determinedly.

—but God never sends you anything you can't handle.

—Amen!

"See Matt?" She nodded at the pierced man. "See that fire over his head?" Matt heard—he twitched as though he had almost reached up to check—and for a second I thought I saw orange flame coiling over his hair like a nest of snakes. I blinked, blinked again. "Doily brains get that glow, right about the time they start to tremble. He'll be trembling soon; you can hear it in his voice sometimes. Then they forget their names, or tell you a story for the twenty-eighth time, or they run their fancy chair right into the wall." Matt flushed. The old woman creaked with malicious laughter. "Fool. Five weeks is nothing." She raised her voice. "It's seven weeks you have to worry about! Seven!" Back to me. "Longer than that and you're stuck with it. Me, I'm just saddled with this damn dog. Ugly son of a bitch. He yaps, and he'll nip if he thinks I'm not paying attention. But if I take care of him he'll trot along sweet as pie till the next time he's tired or hungry or given the wrong food or gets too hot. I just don't forget I'm the boss. You understand me?"

—There's nothing a good attitude can't fix!

She nodded as though I'd said yes, and scratched under her chestnut-colored wig with a bony finger. "Yours, now. Yours ain't a small dog. Not flame, neither. Never seen anything like your great grinning thing."

Grinning thing? Nothing made sense. It was too hot, and too many people were talking at once.

—kind to the world and the world will be kind right back.

"You scared? You should be. It's aiming to kill you. And I doubt you'll stop it."

My chair went over with a *bang*. The group turned as one, their upturned faces blank. "You," I said, but the rest of the words clotted with rage.

I tried to slam the door behind me, but it was on a hydraulic hinge and just wheezed shut slowly over the old woman's laughter.

———

ANGER IS A STRANGE BEAST, hot and burly as a bear. It slumbers in its cave, ignoring all petty distractions until one day along comes someone stupid with a stick. Then anger roars out in a rush of adrenaline. It's a physical thing that needs physical remedies. I needed the punchbag, but I did not want to go to the dojo and face Bonnie. I did not want to face anyone.

By the time I got home I felt drained, and thought maybe the anger was gone for a while. But when an animal leaves its cave, you know it's lived there: there are droppings, and chewed bones that need cleaning out. And that takes words.

A good place for angry words is social media. When there is only a screen, you can get down and nasty and spew bile on the whole human race for *being* whole. And no matter what you say, or when—four in the morning, lunchtime, eight o'clock at night—someone, somewhere, will be listening and have an opinion. Or several.

Rip settled on my lap and I went hunting. The first hashtag I found, #MSproud, was a crew of chirpy cripples filling their posts with anodyne encouragement, emojis and gifs of their "fur babies," and of grandkids who could not be bothered to visit. As I read I breathed faster and faster and now the rage was back like a living thing humping its way up my throat. When I read <My

wife never complained about her malady. Her struggle was an inspiration for us all!> I wanted to use my hands like killing tools. I threw the tablet so hard it bounced off the sofa and onto the rug. Rip purred. She was a predator; in her world violence was meat and drink.

The alarm on my phone pinged: time for my shot.

I took ranitidine to protect my stomach against naproxen, then took the naproxen against the muscle aches of Rebif, then pulled down my pants, reached around awkwardly, and stuck the full 22 mg in my ass. It hurt. First thing tomorrow I'd need the modafinil to fight through the fatigue.

Anger made me restless.

More research. More rage. And I began to see a pattern. From the freezer I got a gel pack—the one I used to use for training injuries—to sit on. Back to Twitter. I used the #MultipleSclerosis and #disability hashtags, added, with bitter fuck-you pride, one of my own, #CripRage, and began a storm of tweets.

<I have multiple sclerosis. MS is not a gift sent by god to improve me. It will not make me humble.>

<I'm not a sweet crip here to inspire you. I'm not here to be liked. I won't disguise my impairment to make you think I'm just like you.>

<I'm not just like you. I have MS. I have a hole in my spinal cord. There is no cure. But there are plenty of drugs to choose from.>

<Drugs that cost more per year than the median annual household income. They work—if they work—by "mechanism unknown.">

<All have terrible side effects. Many cause real damage. Some will kill you. But don't worry!>

<Big Pharma will sell you drugs to treat the damage. And then drugs to treat that drug damage too.>

<Big Pharma makes money off our backs and AMSS makes money off Big Pharma. More than $120m p.a. How much goes direct to people with MS? $10m.>

<AMSS spends the rest on useless counselors and a magazine full of Big Pharma ads: the AMSS exists only to perpetuate itself.>

<Why do we not have control of our own medical process and funding? Why aren't we in charge? Why isn't MS World like HIV?>

<One, money. When HIV groups first formed, there were no drugs, so no money. PWAs and their allies did it for themselves.>

<Two, gender bias. Four times more women than men get MS. And women in this world don't have control.>

<We're treated as objects. We're treated as weak. We're *supposed* to be weak. We learn to *believe* we're weak.>

<But an impairment is not something to be ashamed of. MS is not a moral blight, it's a disease.>

<If you have MS: YOU ARE NOT WEAK. YOU ARE NOT A LESSER BEING. Next time someone calls something *lame* punch them in the fucking throat.>

<You are not pitiful, not useless. You are real. We are real. Real people, with real feelings, real desires, real thoughts.>

<We have holes in our spines and holes in our brains but we're still whole human beings, full citizens of our society.>

<We need money, not just for research, which all goes to Big Pharma anyway. We need money for living: for ramps, for wheelchairs, for vans—>

<—for meds that work. For quality of life. We *don't* need pity. We *don't* need homilies. We need action. Now.>

<MS is my experience but I bet some of this applies to others. If you're Deaf or visually impaired or look different—>

<—you probably know what I'm talking about. So RT if you get it and want to do something about this. Contact me. My DMs are open.>

Then I collected the tweets and turned them into a Storify, into a Facebook post, into a series of screenshots, and cross-posted to every platform I could think of.

I GOT UP AT FIVE THE NEXT MORNING to check my messages. There were more than three hundred.

< . . . and why isn't there an organization that helps with homecare, the way the Denver Breast Cancer project does here?> from Moke in Denver.

< . . . so tired of having to explain that I'm not stupid, just Deaf> raged Kali in Kansas.

<Yes! Yes! Let's set up a group now! Today!> nothing-nothing in Eureka, California.

<Nothing about us without us!> from RageWith-aMachine, planet earth.

I scrolled through them all, tears running down my cheeks.

MODAFINIL TURNED OUT TO BE JUST WHAT I NEEDED to ride the social media wave: a narcolepsy drug like a smooth, high-tech version of meth. I set up *Cripples Action Team*. CAT was a great acronym. Fast, powerful, ruthless, and in-your-face uncompromising. Inside forty-eight hours we had four hundred members and a tagline: *Whatever it takes to help us help ourselves.* I liked *Nothing about us without us!* better, but it was already taken. In a blaze of energy, I put up a website, CAT-org.com, with a single page: the tagline, a contact form, and a big blue Donate button that went to a newly opened bank account. We could tweak it later. I drafted a mission statement and sent out a link to the document for members to tear down and rebuild. Then I started calling people: activists first, and those who thought of themselves as the leaders of the local social justice community. They gave me time because they still recognized my name. And I was involved in the search for a new director for GAP, the plum job.

I used much of the same spiel I put in the original post.

"—and we need money. We need time and attention. We *don't* need pity. Empathy, yes. Help, yes. Pity, never.

You feel sorry for me? Donate. Right now. Do it. Crips are more than twenty percent of all voters. We're a powerful bloc. Send me a thousand dollars. You're over budget? Then donate office equipment . . ." I would sell the good stuff, barter the rest, but they didn't need to know that.

I wrote to Aiyana.

> Fund-raising's all about leverage. You should have seen me: on the phone round the clock with producers at WSB and Fox 5 to get stories out. Then links to those stories on the website. Then press releases about the website. I bullied Max to get the mayor to let me use his name in a letter. You remember that time we went to Bacchanalia but the wait was too long? Two lunches and a dinner meeting there—fuck, it is not cheap—and I had the Chamber of Commerce. And from there it was a sweet, smooth glide to the big dogs of corporate Atlanta: Coca-Cola, Delta, UPS. We are in business!

The mission statement began to take shape:

> CAT is a flexible task force with an active, evolving mission to help disabled people help ourselves. Whatever a specific community needs.

Flexible was important. I'd watched too many non-profits fall foul of IRS exemption rules when their mission changed slightly.

Currently, we prioritize:

- Providing low-cost, practical quality-of-life services to people with disabilities.
- Lobbying to improve local, regional, and national legislation affecting people with disabilities. (Team with National ADAPT on this?)
- Training in media networking to maintain a voice in any issue relating to disabled lives, including but not limited to transport, education, healthcare, working conditions, minimum wage. "Nothing about us without us!"
- Connecting networks: home healthcare, medical advocacy, voter registration, and more! We envision this changing, sometimes rapidly, in response to need.

I opened a new PO Box for public correspondence and filled in the paperwork to incorporate as a Georgia nonprofit. That required a street address. I hesitated. I was reluctant to use my own address because the data was subject to FOI requests. But few people bothered with FOI, and I needed speed. I used my address. As the federal healthcare law was currently written, pre-existing conditions were no longer a problem for individually purchased insurance. But that could revert anytime. I needed to get CAT's finances steady enough to hire employees. Employees meant group health insurance. And small group health insurance could obviate the pre-existing condition problem. I had ten months before my current plan ran out.

ROSE CAME BY THE SAME DAY that I heard CAT had been granted status as a registered nonprofit. "And it's called—what? Cripples Action Team?" We were in the living room. Miz Rip was sitting like a miniature sphinx on her lap, eyes half lidded. "Cripple is an ugly word to call yourself."

"Think of it as reclaiming it." Like *queer*. She hadn't much liked that, either.

"And you've got 501(c)(3) already . . ." Rose was tan, and ten pounds heavier, but there was a dissatisfied look to the rich, smooth skin of her face, one I recognized. She had been bored on that cruise. Miz Rip stood, stretched, turned around, and settled down again in exactly the same position. "You're just like a grown cat already, aren't you?" She stroked Rip under the chin with one finger—

all that would fit. "And I bet you're just like your mom, all ready to fight things ten times your size."

Ten years ago we'd had a hamster for a while. Rose had always talked to it instead of me when she disapproved of something I'd done.

"What is it this time?"

"Nothing." She stroked Rip some more. "I just think you need to look at what exactly you're fighting."

"What do you mean? All this inertia isn't enough for you? How about discrimination? What about—"

"That's not what I mean."

I blinked.

"You're acting the same way you did twelve years ago, when you first started karate and self-defense. As though if you could just find the right lever to pull you could make the world safe."

"That—"

"No. Listen." Her eyes were very bright. "I thought I was going to lose you all those years ago. You were angry all the time. 'Women,' you said. 'We're being hunted like deer!' And off you'd go to the dojo to hit things and dream about hitting people. You never let up. Every movie we saw, you'd shout at the screen, 'Why isn't that woman fighting back!' You'd throw every book you read at the wall: 'Why? Why are they doing this to us?' You saw violence against women everywhere."

"It *is* everywhere."

"So is disease, and starvation, and child abuse. We don't change our lives because of it. All those drills you made me do: what to do if I was in the kitchen and you were in the bedroom and a man with a knife came in. What to do if I were held hostage. And you'd get angry at me if I protested." I didn't remember that. "I tried to talk to you but you couldn't see, you *wouldn't* see, that you were so angry because you were scared. And now you're scared again. I don't blame you. MS is a scary thing. A terrible thing. Fear is understandable. So is anger. But not this kind of anger, this awful, burning rage that just feeds on itself. You need to *accept* what's happened."

"I don't—"

"No. I don't mean give up or give in, just . . . Mara, you're frightening me."

I didn't want to frighten her. I hadn't known that I had frightened her before.

CAT's full of cripples, that's what people see, but cripple is just one facet of a person's existence. We're also marketing gurus, code monkeys, project managers . . . A few are crips but not sick and tired—and I have modafinil. It's amazing how fast you can set up a test org when you expect it to not work. When you think, Hey, whatever doesn't work we'll just fix. We worked full-on, all day and half the night, and got the skeleton up—a slick website, complete with funding, sponsorship from a pet-walking app, and partnership with an animal shelter—to get pets to crips who live alone. The pets, dogs mostly, are for adoption, or short stay, or just a two-hour visit. It's called PAWS—Pets As Warm Support. Let Gospa sue.

I did not tell her about the old woman. I did not tell her about Rose. I only told her the parts that would make me sound vital and active. Alive. Worth coming home to.

The test org was meant to serve Metro Atlanta, but things moved too fast to stay small. Once I had had my fortieth message from places like Athens, and Columbus, and Augusta, I called together a CAT quorum and we rewrote the PAWS charter for all of Georgia. Then, of course, I started getting calls from Alabama and Tennessee. Who didn't want a two-hour visit from a friendly puppy that you didn't even have to take for a walk? Soon I was going to need an admin assistant.

The sky was bright but temperatures unpredictable: thirty-one degrees one day with air hard as a plate, a soft seventy-two the next. I ignored it all, and got busier and busier, and woke up more often with my legs not quite working and the stretched-tight feeling of exhaustion and nausea. I couldn't seem to stop. I could take more pills, but what I really needed was a break, to get out under the sky.

THE LAST DAY OF JANUARY felt almost normal: gray and fifty, the kind of weather that made Atlantans stay at home. The north end of Lake Lanier was quiet and still: a combination of the cold and drought-level depth made it difficult to launch a boat, and kept the fishing tours and partyers away.

My still-water kayak weighed less than twenty-five pounds and folded up into a box with a strap. With no one around I could park by the water and drag it to the sloping, red-dirt shore. Even working slowly, with rests, it took less than twenty minutes to unfold, snap into its pointed twelve-foot shape, and tighten. All I could hear were a few birds and the lap of the water against the big rock I would use to get in. By the time I buckled on my life vest and decided what angle to feather my blades I was already tired, but the tension between my shoulders had eased.

Without a dock, it was harder to get into a still-water kayak than a sea kayak, and it meant getting wet. But that's what the wet suit was for.

The water was cold and heavy. But within two minutes my arms and shoulders remembered the rhythm, and the kayak's bow began to slip through the water. I left the dirt and bare alders behind and headed into the deeper channel that sixty years ago had been the Chattahoochee River.

I rested the paddle across the cockpit rim and drifted. Under the surface swam bass and bluegill. On the shore of the wilder areas there might be bear and beaver, and before now I had seen duck and deer, but today all I saw was gray sky and gray water. Here I could forget that walking was hard. There was no one looking, no one to guess my legs did not work. It was just me under the sky.

Then I realized how far the shore was, the effort it would take to paddle back. I would not have the juice to climb out of the boat, drag it up the slope, pack it up, pack it out, drive myself home.

JANUARY TURNED TO FEBRUARY and the weather skated from one extreme to the other. I could walk well enough if I moved slowly. One Saturday morning I headed down McLendon, enjoying the sun on my face. People in bright spring colors, blue and salmon and yellow, strolled on the sidewalk, nodding and smiling behind their sunglasses. At the Flying Biscuit I had to wait ten minutes amid the bright brunch world of friends and couples for my latte to go. Outside, the angle of the light was too low, picking out shadows from the mellow brick and root-heaved sidewalk that were all wrong, and the trees were bare. I could not shake the feeling that this was not my world.

Emails from Aiyana were bright and fast and far away.

> Summer school almost over. Man, they *work* over here! xx

And

> Planning for new school year, starts in just 2 weeks. Busy as hell. xx

The one picture she sent showed her lithe and strong and smiling. Smiling.

Miz Rip grew, snowdrops showed green above the dirt, and Rose came by less often. I found myself wondering who now owned that beautiful kayak I had left on the shore. There had been no phone signal by the lake, no way to call for help. By the time I got halfway home I was too tired, and too ashamed of my own weakness, to call anyone. When I went back the next day the kayak was gone.

GAP got a new director—not the one I would have chosen. I had lunch with Christopher.

"He's a bitch," he said unhappily. "I don't think I'll be able to stay." He poured more dressing on his salad. "How about your new project? Any openings there?"

"Yes, if you can work on a month-to-month contract for a while. The money's not stable yet. We have to get that sorted. And find some work space."

"You have extra space in your home."

"No." I wanted to get the MS work out of my house. Draw a line between me and it. "I'd rather be around people. It's what I'm used to."

We talked more about the new ED—he was making all the wrong choices about client data security, opting for the low bid I had rejected; and he had locked horns with Hernandez about the Hate Crimes Task Force, trying to play the naked influence card instead of cloaking it decently in Atlanta good-old-boy geniality. "I heard him. He called him 'Hernandez'—didn't even bother with 'Captain'—and said, 'Hey, my buddy the mayor will take my side on this.'"

The mayor did not have buddies; he had sycophants and underlings. More to the point, Christopher was right: Hizzoner was a stickler for chain of command. He wouldn't fuck with the chief, and the chief would back her man Hernandez. The only way to persuade her of anything was to buy her bourbon and talk about the old days when she was a vice cop. I learned that from my first self-defense teacher—to persuade an adversary, talk to them in their language and tell them the story they want to hear. But my old self-defense teacher was in Seattle, and GAP was no longer my problem.

We talked about nothing in particular for the rest of the meal.

What I had told Christopher was true. I had to get the group's finances on track. The first six months of a nonprofit are crucial. After the initial three-month surge of memberships, media interest, and donations of time and money, there is always a lull. We had a benefit dinner and a sponsored walk scheduled for next month, but this month we were short more than three thousand dollars.

The next day, I called the bank. They were sympathetic but unhelpful: no assets, no line of credit. "You let GAP overdraw three months in a row early last year," I pointed out.

"That's not usual practice."

"But you did it."

"Our policies have changed."

I doubted it. It was just that GAP had a lot of powerful, public figures on its side and was run by professionals they knew. CAT was a fledgling organization without much clout. Yet. "I'm prepared to be personally responsible for the debt incurred." The money would come in next month.

Tick-tick of keys. "I'm afraid your income does not meet our requirements for a loan." You're no longer one of us.

I thumbed the phone off and resisted the urge to throw it. Miz Rip mewled, then mewled again more piteously when I refused to play with the piece of string that was her favorite toy.

"Assets, Miz Rip. What can I use as assets?" She patted her string hopefully, then stalked off into the kitchen. Her tag clinked against her food bowl as she ate.

Cat food. Of course. All those people served by PAWS. Tens of thousands. A very specific group. A very specific mailing list.

I SENT OUT AN INVITE for CAT's task force—I'd become allergic to the term "Executive Committee"—to conference on WebEx. For this conversation, email and Slack would not do.

"We already deliver pet food to owners' homes, free of charge, but our PAWS users might also need flea spray, pet-sitting services, name tags, collars, pet-grooming. With members' permission we could offer the list to other vendors. Say a pet-supply store." I waited for Kali's speech-to-text app to catch up. "And think about it, if a client's being served by PAWS, they'd probably also be interested in other specialty delivery services: pharmacy, food, home help."

"You mean sell the list," Moke said.

"We do need money, and it's a salable asset. Think of it as extending our service."

"But everyone on that list would be exposed!" Kali typed.

"Exposed to services they might want," I said. After a moment her face got that set look.

Moke said, "When you say exposed, Kali, are you saying we should hide the fact that we're cripples?"

Kali could not hear Moke's tone but she could see the challenge on their face. After a moment she shook her head and typed, "No. No, of course not."

"We'd only sell to thoroughly vetted organizations," I said. "And we'll build in every safeguard."

"What kind of safeguards?" Doug asked.

"I have experience with client data security," I said. Which was at least adjacent to the truth, and in my tenure at GAP we never had a breach. And this would only be temporary, just until CAT's finances stabilized enough to support permanent employees and qualify for group insurance. "But maybe you and Kali could also do some research on that."

"Sure, I could do some vetting," Kali typed. Moke snorted, but Kali was already typing again. "No pun intended!"

We went back and forth but in the end the task force voted yes. The full membership would follow our recommendations; they always did.

THE DAY AFTER I SIGNED the month-to-month contract with Christopher, my phone chimed with a message from the Justice Institute.

<The theme of this year's conference in Fort Lauderdale is disability. Our original guest speaker has dropped out due to ill health. As the president of a new, vital organization, would you be prepared to deliver a keynote address on short notice?>

It would be a golden opportunity to take us national. *To stay busy and angry*, the Rose in my head whispered. *To not face your fear.*

<Yes>, I thumbed.

<Confirmation to follow.>

I BOUGHT A FOLDABLE TRAVEL CANE, drove myself to the airport, and parked. Climbed out of the car. Realized I would not be able to walk all the way to the ticket counter with my carry-on and stood, feeling foolish, with my bag at my feet and the car door still open. The sky was dark with cloud and far too close. Atlanta had remembered it was still February.

Okay. Just drive to the park-and-ride. There are buses there that will pick you up. No walking. Easy.

Except I was terrified. *What will you do if the bus doesn't come?* Use the phone. *What if your phone doesn't work?* I could drive home and call the Justice Institute. *What if the car breaks down?* My air was running out. I couldn't breathe properly. *What if the car breaks down on the interstate in one of those dead spots?*

It began to rain. I tried to stay calm. I knew this trap. It was like my first self-defense lessons: *What if the man has a knife?* And when the instructor had shown me how to defend against a knife, I wanted to know, *What if he has a gun?* After she addressed that, I asked, *What if there are three of them?* At which point she laughed and told me that she had no idea how to defend against a tank or a nuclear missile, either, and if I thought learning self-defense could ensure perfect safety, I should ask for my money back. There was no such thing. There was always someone bigger, faster, better armed than you. Learn what you can, then improvise.

The clouds thinned abruptly and the wet asphalt gleamed in the weak February sunshine. Do what you can. I could get a cheap spare phone. A backup charger. A signal booster. Always keep the car in good repair. What would I have done before MS if I'd broken down on I-85 without a phone? Walking on the interstate with cars hurtling past was not safe for anyone of any fitness level. I would have figured it out. I would have coped. Rose was wrong; I could face my fears.

Nonetheless, I was almost giddy with relief when the minibus pulled into the parking lot. I laughed too hard at the driver's joke about rain and runways, but I supposed he was used to nervous passengers. He dropped me off right outside the Delta check-in. It was less than a hundred yards to the counter and felt like a mile uphill. I was beginning to weave by the time I got there.

"Tagarelli, Mara," I said, and gave her my driver's license and confirmation number.

She gave me back the license. "I'll call for your chair." She picked up her phone.

"I'm sorry, what?"

"Your wheelchair, ma'am. I'll have to call for it."

The Justice Institute, of course. They would have arranged it. Probably just transferred the arrangements for their previous guest to me. After all, all disabled people were the same. I was still blinking at her when the chair trundled up, pushed by a porter.

"She needs gate A-17." She handed the porter my ticket.

He nodded at the chair for me to sit down. "Time's the flight?" he asked the ticket agent.

"Two thirty-five." She handed him my boarding pass.

"She got baggage to check?"

She. As though I were not there. The porter picked up my bag, slung it over his shoulder and nudged the chair at me—just an inch, he probably didn't even know he was doing it, but between one breath and the next I had no choice. He had my ticket and my bag. I and my wants were no longer part of the equation.

I was tired, and this was all new to me. I sat.

He pushed me through the busy concourse, nodded to the woman at the security gate. She nodded back to him—I did not exist—and unhooked the barrier ribbon, and he shoved me through to the head of the line. I wondered if they would even hear me if I told them I'd changed my mind, that I didn't want to fly after all.

"Female assist!" the male TSA agent bellowed. "Female assist!" The porter gestured for my shoes, put them and my bag in a gray tray, and vanished through the line of scanners. All around me children with runny noses, adult men without shoes, and women with squalling babies bumped into each other, got in the wrong line, took the wrong bag on the other side of the scanner. One man ran right into me as though I wasn't there. A woman hit me in the head with her swinging diaper bag, then glared at me as though I were the problem.

No shoes, no boarding pass, no bag, no phone. I was stuck and no one had bothered to give me a clue how long I'd be here. What if I missed my flight?

Another jolt, but this time it was a TSA agent trying without warning to push the chair. She huffed, bent past me, and flicked off the brakes.

"I'm eight minutes past my time," she shouted to another agent as she rammed me through the swinging glass gate.

"Not my fault," he said.

"Well, all the other handicapped can miss their plane," she called over her shoulder. "After this one, I'm done."

She wheeled me past an area where people were putting on their shoes.

"You been through this before?" Extra loud, extra slow. "You want privacy?"

While I was wondering why I would need privacy she pulled on blue gloves, said, "Hold out your arms," and began patting me down.

So much for choice.

"Lean forward." A cursory touch of my back. "Lean back." Even more cursory pat down my front. "Lift your right leg. Left." Then she swiped a piece of paper over the arms of the chair, fed it into a machine, waited, and at the green light stripped off the gloves and tossed them and the paper into a bin already half full.

"Good to go!" she shouted to no one in particular, and stumped off.

That was it? I could have been sitting on a bomb or an Uzi. I imagined the oiled heft of an Uzi; SWAT teams running; my red-splattered corpse on CNN and a witness voiceover sobbing, "She was screaming about being treated like a sack of potatoes." And then the porter handed me my shoes.

The airport looked different from a wheelchair. We traveled through the bowels of the building, the mysterious world of the passkey and freight elevator. No carpets down here. No neon. All gray, all concrete, with pools of yellow-white light, and deathly quiet, apart from the rattle and squeak of the decrepit chair. The porter did not say a single word. I was just baggage. I wondered if he thought about how helpless I was; how much at his mercy I might be.

I had been in a chair before, of course, when I was first training as a counselor. To see how it felt. Then, I could get up anytime and call a halt. This was different. This was as though the chair had turned me invisible, written me out of the story. I began to understand why all those people at the AMSS group were so defeated.

LEAVING THE TERMINAL in Fort Lauderdale was like walking into an Atlanta summer: moisture thick enough to stand on that tightened around me like plastic wrap, the kind of air you have to sip rather than breathe. The hotel could have been any conference hotel in North America; I had never realized how far the walk was from drop-off to reception, from reception to the elevator, the elevator to the room. I had never been in an accessible room before: wet room rather than the usual tub and shower, sinks and counters low and weirdly skeletal looking, pipes exposed to permit wheelchair users to get in close. But it was spacious, I liked that. I unpacked and went down to registration.

Academic or organizational conferences centered on social justice form a two-sided ecosystem, like the ocean on either side of an equatorial thermocline: the well-lit layer where professionals bask and sport above the dim reach of the slow-moving clients—or constituents or stakeholders, members or customers, special interest group or community, depending on the agency and the year. What never changed was the dynamic. The conference was organized around those at the top of the food chain, who made their living from those below. If you ran a nonprofit, or wrote papers about those who needed the services of a nonprofit, you floated in the warmth of power and influence. You were approached by corporate reps and interviewed for jobs, you hung out in the bar in good clothes and laughed with the journalist who had just sucked dry an angry, badly dressed member of the latest social justice struggle then tossed the husk back into the cold, oxygen-starved depths.

As the executive director of the Georgia AIDS Partnership I'd swum in the dappled warmth, seeing and being seen. I was sought after and had access to those I sought. When the U.S. Conference on AIDS moved from one rich metropolis to another, D.C. to L.A. to New York, I moved with it, easy and untroubled. Every now and again I joined the larger shoal at the International AIDS Society in Durban or Melbourne, Rio or Vienna.

The JI conference was not like that. I had been expecting some difference—it was a much smaller affair than USCA or IAS, and I did not have a long schedule of appointments and private meetings—but I had not really understood that I now belonged on the other side of the divide. I was a crip, not one of the real people. My purpose was to be brought up from the deep, exhibited, and cast back.

For those in the warmer waters close to the surface, the big late-night, bar-based, strange-city conference teemed with sexual opportunity. I was used to the after-dinner meetings over wine that became a nightcap and moved into just-a-little-too-close, just-a-bit-too-touchy confidences. For most of my time I had been with Rose, and turned aside the propositions briskly or kindly or regretfully, depending. I had not realized that now part of me had been looking forward to the possibility of saying yes, or making my own proposals.

I walked into the bar, deprecating smile ready, but those who looked up eagerly seemed to not see me. The cane outweighed even the special maroon-and-turquoise lanyard on my conference badge and KEYNOTE printed in block letters under my name. Even when I tripped over a woman's purse on the writhing blue-and-white patterned carpet, gazes glided over me as though I were wearing a cloak of invisibility. The bartender saw me but the margarita tasted more sour than usual. When the second person banged into my bar stool without apologizing, my sense of unreality strengthened. The world began to feel insubstantial and treacherous. I ordered another margarita. As the bartender shook it, I heard a whispery laugh at my shoulder and turned slowly. Nothing. But I could not shake the sense that something had dodged out of sight and was mocking me from behind a pillar. It felt like a cruel child's game that played on a human's most atavistic fear: the monster was coming and everyone but you knew its name. You were the scapegoat.

At two in the morning, sleepless, I wrote a long, wandering email to Aiyana about the old woman's Small Dog Theory of illness: keep your illness tended and it won't yap and mess up your life. Only her MS wasn't my MS because what I was going through was not like a small fucking dog. No wonder she's so old if her MS is just a tiny yapping pug. And if she really is so old she's too old for sex, anyway, so what would she care? Or maybe that theory only works if everyone around you is so cowed they ignore the farting drooling vile little yellow-collared fucker . . .

I deleted it. It was ugly, it didn't make sense, and I sounded deranged.

What was Aiyana doing right now? Maybe finishing her workday with a colleague, saying, Want to grab a beer? Sitting in their cutoff shorts, arms draped casually over the back of the wooden bar bench. The smiles that went on just a little too long, bare thighs close enough to feel the warmth, hear the catch of breath, bask inside the carefree scent of each other's healthy body.

WHEN I GOT HOME two days later, the first thing I did was message my neurologist via the clinic's patient portal.

<It's getting harder to walk.>

Liang wrote me an order for physical therapy.

I'd been in PT before, twice, for training injuries. Both were short, focused courses. Brisk and businesslike.

This was not that. Though it probably looked like that from the outside. We did the assessment: "Touch this, lift that." Surprise, surprise, I have MS. Apparently my right peroneus and all three right adductors are weak. No shit. But that wasn't what was weird.

It took me a while to work out what was.

THE THERAPIST, Brian, had been perfectly polite, but it was clear I was of no account, a cripple not a woman, someone he had to touch because it was his job, about as important to him as a chair. For my whole life men's sexual attention had been nothing but an irritating, occasionally exhausting consequence of being alive—like gravity: not something you think about much until it's gone.

The second session was worse.

> He's big. Gentle, like I said, physically anyhow. He had me flat on my back, left leg bent at the knee and right straight up. He was stretching out my hamstring—I hadn't even noticed it was getting tight—pushing until it released, then a bit farther, then holding until it released. It wasn't painful, but it's not exactly comfortable, and it feels dangerous because you're so helpless and one slip would break you in half. Just part of the shit you have to endure at PT. So I was okay, until he said, sort of clinically, "My friend was doing this with a client, a 73-year-old

woman, and something went crunch. He broke her hip." I blinked and he laughed and lowered my leg. Then he took hold of my left, and raised it slowly to its limit, then a little over. "But you know the crazy thing? She came back a month later after a hip replacement and he did it to the other one!"

Aiyana took thirty-six hours to reply.

I don't think he was threatening you. I wonder if he was just repeating an urban legend—did you check Snopes?

I stared at it for a long time. Snopes. So in addition to being an unreliable narrator, now I was a gullible fool, too? I imagined her with her new friends, rolling their eyes at the doily brain's paranoia.

Of course he wasn't threatening me; he didn't think I was worth threatening. She hadn't listened to a word I'd said.

I HAD FORGOTTEN I'D SUBSCRIBED to *MonSter!* until I got an email apologizing for not being able to fulfill my subscription. Despite a "glorious thirty-year run as the beating heart of the MS community," their subscriber base was down ninety-five percent since its nineties heyday—I was surprised at the graphic they included showing that in 1993 its circulation was in the six figures—and due to that and "a series of unfortunate circumstances" they were shutting down, effective immediately. I guessed that meant the founders' health and will had faltered. When I went to their website I got a 404 Not Found message. Another community-based organization gone as tracelessly as a foundered ship.

LIANG DOUBLED MY DOSE of Rebif. I had severe reactions to the increased dose: headaches, muscle spasms, and vomiting. Once, after crouching and puking into a bucket, I lay on the carpet and a purring Rip bumped my sweat-soaked head. I soldiered on grimly. The spasms stopped after a while, and the vomiting. But my legs ached all the time and my brain felt packed in cotton wool. I canceled one then another PT session.

One morning while the kettle boiled I was staring out the window when a flick of red caught my attention. I wandered out onto the back deck. That flick of red again down in the yard. A bird. Crimson with a black beak. And something smelled good, perfumey. There, down by the door to the subbasement we no longer used: a bush with tiny white flowers. I walked down the steps onto the grass: sometime when I was not looking it had turned from straw yellow to fresh minty green. And there were weeds. Was that new or something Rose took care of?

I remembered the kettle and went back inside.

The injection site reactions on my stomach and thighs and buttocks got worse. I worked on CAT business strapped with ice packs now. I began to use a cane whenever I left the house.

There was a message from Doug, the CAT director in Minnesota: one of his state senators had changed their vote on the bill we had been working on. I sent some advice about email-in campaigns. I liked Doug. Sometimes he put together YouTube videos of local political shenanigans in the persona of Inspector Clouseau, complete with hat and glasses, exaggerated fake mustache, and a terrible accent. "Gives me something to do," he said on one of our Skype calls, giving me his curled-to-one-side smile.

Miz Rip leapt onto my lap. I winced. She was bigger, and bored. Maybe I should put a cat flap in the back door. But she wasn't old enough yet.

Not until she is six months old, has all her shots, and been fixed, the vet who gave us a reduced rate for the PAWS account subscribers had said. She also said, *My niece has MS*. She was the fifth person since Christmas to tell me something similar. Why had I never met these people before? Did their friends and relatives keep them locked in the attic? Or did they just turn their faces to the wall and refuse to get out of bed?

"How old are you, anyway?" I asked Rip, then worked it out: eight weeks old when I bought her at Christmas, so born at the beginning of November. Four months ago. When Rose had left. When I first tripped over the leaf that wasn't there.

She was born at the same time as my MS. My MS would live longer.

> Josh is planting tomatoes. He thinks I should grow vegetables. I said, Plant me some flowers. He said, Flowers won't feed you. We settled on some herbs I can grow in pots on the back deck. Easier to take care of. He also tells me I should do yoga. Well, *Apple* thinks I should do yoga. Do I look like an om-and-crystal freak?

Josh was weird but at least he still talked to me. He still saw me.

FEBRUARY'S HINT OF SOFTNESS became March's humid mornings. Spring. The dogwoods and cherry trees were in bloom; their soft pink-and-white clouds fell along every street, and the pavement turned greenish gold with pollen. Green-gold fur collected in the corners of the windows and on the hood of my car.

I was violently allergic to tree pollen. My MS got abruptly worse. Antihistamines did not help. My reactions to the Rebif increased, until by the end of April the hivelike swellings on my legs and stomach started to weep clear serum and it hurt to pull on a pair of jeans. Humidity now stifled the whole day. Good weather to be out on the water, but I had no kayak and could not face the hurly-burly of the boat dock and negotiating a rental.

CAT's revenues were just stable enough to transition Christopher to part-time-employee status. His first task was to research recent cooperative healthcare groups so that as soon as we could afford for me to draw a salary, too, we could both get benefits.

The neurologist took me off Rebif and put me on Tecfidera, an oral drug that cost $66,000 a year. Cursory research showed it was a repurposed German psoriasis drug, which itself was a repurposed furniture fumigant. More than $5,000 a month for a drug that killed pests in furniture. But a pill twice a day was better than needles. And for the first six months at least there would be a co-pay program: the first few hits were free. With the program came membership in a pharma-sponsored MS peer group. Most HIV regimens came with the same marketing and I knew how they operated. One look at the image of a healthy-looking woman leaning on a fence in some Big Sky state told me all I needed. I recycled the brochure without reading it.

Two hours after I swallowed the first pill, I turned hell-red and burned for ninety minutes. And the second time, and the third. On day four, my heart raced away with me. I counted to 180 beats a minute, then could not keep up. Then it eased. On the fifth day, I was making tea when pain flashed down my left arm so bright and sudden that I froze in mid-pour. I breathed carefully but when I tried to move the pain flashed again. After an archery injury ten years ago something like this had happened: pain in my left arm caused by movement. Ulnar and median nerve inflammation, my internist said. I knew how to deal with it. Moving one millimeter at a time, I set the kettle down, edged to the kitchen table, and sat. Normally it was three strides. It took me five minutes.

I sat for nearly an hour, until the pain began to leach away.

The next day I seemed fine: the flushing was minimal, my heart rate no faster than that of someone who had climbed a flight of stairs. But that night, getting undressed while Rip kneaded the bed, nerve signal ripped through my neck and arm, then again before I could catch my breath, and again and again, until it became a sheet of lightning that flashed through my entire left side in an endless cataract of electricity that turned my brain white.

I managed to call 911, but every time I tried to organize my thoughts enough to speak, the pain blew me apart and made me yell. But landlines are wired into the system.

All I remember of the ER was a nightmare of people shouting, another botched IV, and finally fentanyl flowing into me like ice water to freeze the pain in place and float it far away. I went home with a prescription for two oxycodone every six hours.

A nervous system under the influence of serious opiates feels as though it is routing electrical signals through another dimension. I would decide to raise my right hand and, after galaxies moved past each other and stars died, my hand would lift, by which time I'd forgotten what I was reaching for. Every detail became hyperclear and interesting. I found myself seeing a whole world in the grain of the coffee table. Sound slowed and took on substance.

Around six o'clock I realized I'd forgotten to take my morning Tecfidera. I took it with two more lovely round white pills.

As evening came, shadows began to twist and sway. One detached itself from the corner of the door fifteen feet away and crept toward me. I sat and watched. A person, maybe, but a stretched-thin person who wasn't there, who instead of lengthening like a normal shadow grew denser and more defined. The air above it began to thicken as though the shadow were trying to step through to reality.

I licked my lips. I did not like that.

My left arm fizzed tentatively. I did not like that at all.

A ghost of a laugh. Oh, I really did not like that. And then my arm flashed with pain, bright as light, and I tried to move but the pain spiked me to the chair, and again, and again. And I could not take my eyes off that shadow reaching out to me. *It's aiming to kill you—*

—and Rip was hissing, fur raised, and I blinked, and then she was chasing her tail then cleaning her paw and the shadow was just a shadow.

Half an hour later the pain faded to nothing and I got up and turned the lights on, and sat again, watching doors and windows and floors. But nothing moved.

In the morning I took just one oxycodone, and noted the exact time of my Tecfidera dose. Two hours and five minutes later, my heart began to accelerate and the first nerve pain flashed through my arm.

When it passed I phoned Liang's office and told them I was coming in.

I told her about the flushing and increased heart rate. She nodded. "Peripheral nervous system excitation is one of the listed side effects."

I told her about the pain. Its shape and heft and color.

"Interesting," she said.

"It's the drug."

"That's not one of—"

"It's the Tecfidera," I said.

She pondered. "Have you had pain in that arm before?"

"Years ago, after an archery injury—my elbow." She frowned. "But not like this, not endless waves that build and build and then just flood me. It's like someone breaks the dam and all the pain in the world pours out."

"Ah." She sat back. "Pain gating. Pain gate failure."

My turn to frown.

"Do you swim?"

"I have swum." I'd never liked it; too much constant resistance. I preferred sports with moving objects I could hit.

"When you first jump in the pool the cold is shocking. But five minutes later you've forgotten it. That's because your nervous system shunts the discomfort aside. It figures out that the cold isn't dangerous, and closes the pain gate. You don't need the message, so you don't feel it anymore. It's possible that Tecfidera excited your peripheral nervous system to the degree that your pain gate failed. But that's not one of the listed side effects."

"Then we should list it."

"I can report it to the FDA."

"Do."

She nodded. "It could be demyelination of the peripheral . . . Hmm—the überganger zone . . ." She cleared her throat. "I'd like a cervical MRI with contrast. And perhaps we should next consider—"

"No."

She tilted her head to one side. "You might have a new lesion. We really need—"

We. There was no *we* when it came to pain. "No."

"Then another course of pred—"

"No. I'm sick of it all."

Before we moved to this country, when my little sister was two she used to sit in the back garden—the yard—and dig up worms with her hands. When she didn't squash them by mistake she'd drop them in one of those miniature plastic buckets and croon to herself while they hauled their way up the smooth sides to freedom, fighting for every quarter inch. When they got to the top she'd flick them to the bottom again. They kept trying. Over and over. When she got bored she ate them.

I SAT IN THE BACKYARD. It was mid-morning but clouds were already gathering and the air tightening: thunderstorm weather. Miz Rip stalked a swaying weed. It was only her second time outside; she adapted frighteningly fast. She was still young, of course; her brain still elastic, still forming its neural networks. My brain was set in its ways. And now there were holes in it.

I lay on the grass and stared at the clouds gathering like silverfish. I wondered how it would feel to surrender like vapor to the wind, let go, give in. I could throw myself in front of a car. But that was a little melodramatic, and there was the driver to consider. A fall from a tall building would work. Carbon monoxide—but I would hate that awful exhaust stink to be the last thing I smelled. Pills. I had a lot of those now. Rose would miss me, but she had Louise. CAT could stagger along on its own. It was healthy enough financially since I started selling the mailing lists. There was nothing to stop me really. My mother would be upset, but she had survived the loss of her other daughter. She hadn't seen me in nearly a year, hadn't even visited after the diagnosis, and it seemed too hard to travel to London now. Aiyana might never come back.

I plucked a blade of grass idly. My life wasn't mine anymore, anyway, it was the disease's.

Miz Rip jumped onto my chest. She'd brought me a dandelion. Its scent was fresh and sharp; the stem oozed slightly. Rip smelled exactly like herself: dusty sunshine. A bird sang. I blinked hard. It was a lovely day. Really.

MAY WAS HOT. From my air-conditioned car to the air-conditioned co-working space was only ten yards, but the pavement wavered in the heat and my cane seemed to sink into the blacktop. A man I passed at the door pretended not to see me struggle. The woman behind the reception desk smiled in a bright Southern way, as impersonal as dropping a coin in a beggar's cup; before the cane she'd greeted me by name.

At his designated desk, Christopher was happily tapping away. "The latest FDA proposals are in Dropbox." He looked at me more closely. "Are you all right?"

I propped my cane against the windowsill and sat. "I've been better." I opened Dropbox and tried to pay attention to the FDA's proposal to tighten their accelerated drug approval procedures, but I was so tired that the words eeled out of my grasp. I pushed the laptop away, baffled, and decided to tackle email.

I worked for two hours, until even simple email sentences began to elude me. When I started hitting the wrong keys, I gave up. "I'm done," I said to Christopher. Iced coffee would help, but the thought of struggling onto one of the high bar stools in the café while everyone studiously looked away seemed like too much work. "I'm going home."

I made my way home through the fudgy heat. The sky was clear but there would be a storm mid-afternoon,

I could feel it. I watched an old Star Trek movie. Ate ice cream.

The mail came. A letter from my mother, handwritten, which was her way of saying *I love you* without having to do much, and four pieces of junk mail—two with one of the false middle initials I'd put in to track who was using our mailing list. Also an invitation to donate to a women's foundation in Eureka, California. I tossed the fund-raiser in the recycling. Skimmed the letter from my mother: more complaints about the unfairness of life. Looked at the junk mail. One of the envelopes with my false initial came from a cane and stick manufacturer. It was a nice brochure. But we hadn't sold our list to this company.

I phoned Christopher. "Who got the list with the initial *J*?"

Faint ticking of the keyboard. "Pet People."

"Send them an email: we know they're selling the list on. Tell them not to do it again, that we want the entire proceeds of that secondary sale, and that if we don't have a satisfactory reply from them in ten working days we contact our attorney."

"Feeling better?"

"Ice cream has a way of pepping a girl up." On cue, the spoon in my dish rattled. Rip, licking up the melted remains. I sighed. "Got to go, Christopher." Milk and cream gave her the runs.

The house was strange with storm light and swollen with humidity despite the AC. The air felt menacing, greasy, and electric. Dense charcoal and purple clouds began to layer overhead. It would be a big one. In the gathering dark I went round the house to turn off lights and unplug power strips. Rip followed me, winding in and out of my ankles, getting in the way.

I was pulling the power cord from the bedroom wall when lightning sliced the clouds open and two seconds later the *crack* sent Rip under the bed. Another blinding flash, then another, and in the kitchen the appliances seemed to leap from the dark in vivid freeze-frames. The crack and thunder rolled into one another, with more saber cuts of light until it was like being in the middle of the Charge of the Light Brigade. Then a high BANG and a green-and-violet flash: a transformer going down. And rain fell out of the sky like God had upended a bucket.

When the rain began to steady and there was a gap between crack and rumble, I opened the windows. Cool air gushed through the house. The electricity would not be back for a couple of hours. I plugged a few things back in for when it was and took my iPad to the sofa. With wifi down there was no point trying to stream a show, so instead I pulled up *An Indigenous Peoples' History of the United States* and began to read. Rip crept out from under the bed and settled on my lap. We sat quietly in the cool, earth-scented air and listened to the rain.

I woke to CNN.

"—sclerosis." I scrabbled for the remote and turned up the sound. "Police in Richfield, Minnesota, say they think he was tortured by two or possibly three intruders over a period of twenty-four hours. We go live now to . . ."

My skin felt two sizes too small, as though it was shrinking on my bones.

Switch to live reporter. "—from Richfield, where the local community is in shock. The wheelchair-bound victim"—flash to picture of blond-haired man with a neat mustache, wearing tux and bow tie, laughing at someone off camera—"Karl D. Brawn, was tied into his chair, then systematically beaten, burned, and stabbed. Police report evidence of salt in the victim's wounds." *Karl's wounds*, I thought fiercely. *His name was Karl.* "I asked the spokeswoman about this."

Cut to earlier tape. "So you think the salt was an imaginative torture method?"

Imaginative? Little Johnny is so imaginative . . .

The police spokeswoman, about thirty, white, shrugged. "It's possible, but it might have been a way to check if the victim was unconscious. He probably passed out several times. They would have been checking to see if he reacted. To make sure he was dead."

The reporter nodded as though this were an everyday thing. Normal to comment on torture technique, as though it was baseball. And then CNN turned its avid eyes to the suffering of the marine life off the coast of California, where there had been another oil spill, but I didn't hear it. My senses were turned inward, imagining.

Three men went into another man's house, a man with MS, to rob it. When they found how helpless he was *wheeling himself about the kitchen, wondering whether he needed to buy bread?* they laughed and looked at one another *while he panicked, while he held out his hands, saying "No. Just take the money"* and formed a triangle around him. "Cri-pple," they sang out. "Hey, cri-pple." They would have teased him first, the way groups of men tease young women they are about to rape. The way cats play with their prey. Maybe they pushed his wheelchair this way and that *until tears rolled down his cheeks and he tried to stop crying because he knew it would only make it worse the way it had when he was seven in the schoolyard. They would laugh and poke and jeer and call names and then get disgusted and the pokes would become pushes and the pushes slaps* until they worked themselves up enough to get serious. To find electrical wire in the toolbox and tie him to the chair, to heat the flat of a knife blade in the stove flame and, maybe a little nervous at first, press it against the tender flesh of his inner arm *and he cried out, but they didn't like that, they hit him, and now he swore and spat and they told him to shut up, but he didn't, he couldn't, no he wouldn't because by now he knew they were going to kill him* and when he wouldn't shut up they laid the hot knife across his mouth.

I could imagine the singed smell of mustache hair and cooking lip, the bubbling noise, the shriek, the way it felt as the knife tore away.

I huddled on the floor. The flashing television light shimmered from the walls and licked under the couch, under the table, into every nook and cranny until there was nowhere to hide and I felt as though I was drowning.

THE HOUSE WAS SEALED and the AC on high. I cooked myself lamb chops for dinner, but when I cut into them and saw the blood, I couldn't eat. Rip licked at the blood, but wouldn't touch the meat.

I drank three beers, one after the other, until I felt that fizzing fuzz in my forebrain, but I didn't relax. I ran myself a bath. *Don't be silly*, I told myself as I bobbed in the warm water, *Minnesota is twelve hundred miles away*. Oh, *but*, said a little voice inside, *but* . . .

IT'S AIMING TO KILL YOU. Rip smiles, the way cats cannot. I shudder. *It's aiming to kill you*. And then Rip's face changes and it's the murdered man from Minnesota smiling and saying, "Mara, the senator still isn't taking our calls," and his mustache turns into a caterpillar that humps off his lip and onto the microphone he is using to speak, his hair is darkening and his face is changing, getting older, thinner—

I woke and surged upright. The senator. A man in a wheelchair, mustache neatly shaved off and hair its natural gray-stippled brown, pointing out for the camera—for me—who was who at the fund-raiser in Minneapolis, in *Richfield*, a suburb of Minneapolis. *Douglas*. Add a few years, put him in a chair, take off his mustache, grow out the dyed hair. *Karl D. Brawn.*

Oh God.

I pulled on a T-shirt and scrolled back through CAT email. The latest memo from Minnesota was signed *D*. I went back a few weeks. *Doug*. And before that: *Doug Braun*. Braun, not Brawn. In the eerie blue glow of my screen, the skin on my arms looked grayish. Like a corpse.

I searched Facebook and there he was: Karl Douglas Braun. The photo CNN had used was a throwback profile picture. He must have posted it recently. Doug.

His lover had died sixteen years ago from HIV accelerated by leishmaniasis picked up in Texas. Doug thought some miracle had protected him from HIV—and then he was diagnosed with MS. Some miracle, he'd said. There were good treatments for HIV now. For MS, not so much. He had been fighting back, like me, climbing the wall of the bucket, but trying wasn't enough. It was never enough. To the animals who beat and tortured and killed him it didn't matter how close he had come to swinging the Minnesota senatorial vote. He was just a cripple. Trying didn't matter. What was the point? They got you in the end. He had been so proud of his lightweight chair, his specially adapted van, "I'm doing pretty good," he had said from his driveway, tilting his phone to horizontal to show his van. "I can go buy my own toys now, and meet my Grindr hookups." And he gave me an ironic grin. He had told me a while ago that he had never used a dating app in his life. "No need," he'd said. "A thoracic lesion took care of that stuff years ago." But he did flirt. So alive. So adamant. Refusing to bow his head. Until those idiot children came along and . . . murdered him. To them, he was just a queer cripple. With a target tattooed on his forehead.

AROUND DAWN THE NEXT DAY, I looked up a home security company and phoned them at eight. "I want a monitored system."

Their representative came out that morning. My legs were so stiff I had to use the cane to get to the door. When I opened it the air was already thick with moisture. He had a big neck and sweated heavily. Once in the living room, he put his briefcase down by his feet and looked at the ceiling and walls. "Well, your infrared scanning system is the most secure"—he pronounced it see-cure—"but you got the pet." He pointed his tablet at Miz Rip, who was looking at him suspiciously from the couch. "It'd set the alarms off ten times a day. Lessen of course you keep it outside at night."

"She. No." I leaned on my cane. "She's got her own door. Comes and goes as she pleases."

He shook his head. "Then it'll have to be touch sensors on the doors and windows." Winn-ders. He shook his head again.

"They aren't any good?"

"Oh, they're good, just not *as* good. Course, they are less expensive. If that's the kind of thing that worries you."

I could imagine him in a funeral home, sniffing loudly and sighing when the freshly bereaved wanted something less than the craftsman-made polished mahogany with genuine silk lining and solid brass handles. I knew he was just doing his best to get a fatter commission, but what if Doug had had a system that wasn't good enough? "Do you have any literature on the subject?"

"Yes, ma'am." He picked up his briefcase and walked to the dining room table. "Mind if I set?" He didn't wait for my permission. He splayed three different brochures in front of me. "Now, this here's your top-of-the-line, no-expense-spared system. The—"

I limped over. "I'm sorry. Perhaps I wasn't clear. I want to read them at my leisure, think about it a little."

"Yes, ma'am," he said, "but we could all save some time if you'd just look at—"

"No. I want to read them for myself."

He smiled in that salesman way that meant he wasn't listening to a word I said. "Surely, ma'am. I need to make a phone call, anyhow." He whipped an enormous phone from his briefcase and hit a number before I could say anything.

"Steve!" he said. "Got those specs from the Dunwoody job this morning. Sure. Right here. No problem."

He seemed to be settling down for a long conversation. I wanted him to leave. *What would I do if he refused?* That huge neck. Those big hands. My bad leg and thin stick.

"Uh-huh, uh-huh." He watched me with his beady eyes while he listened to whoever was on the other end of the phone. It occurred to me that if he wanted to enter a woman's house in the middle of the night, he had the perfect job.

This was ridiculous. His company knew he was here. He needed my business to make money. And he had been rude. "I want you to leave," I said.

"Hold on, Steve." He tucked the phone against his chest. "Ma'am?"

"I would like you to leave." I bent and picked up his briefcase, held it out until he took it.

"But, ma'am, if you'll just—"

"You will leave now." I limped to the front door and held it open.

He stood up. "I'll call back tomorrow."

"No. I'll call your office when and if I'm ready to talk to someone."

He left, loosening his collar and looking perplexed. If I had had the coordination, I would have kicked him.

I called another company. "And send a woman, assuming you have any working for you."

The woman who came turned out to be the owner of the local franchise. She was brisk and businesslike, and utterly silent as she looked over the place.

"Will having sensors on the doors and windows be good enough?"

"Unless you think someone wants to try to come through the wall or down the chimney." She smiled. A joke. Relief broke over me. Of course. They weren't superhuman.

Maybe her company was generally more efficient, or maybe I got special treatment, but I had the system— double deadbolts on every door, twist keys on the windows, and their app on my phone—installed the next day. I tapped in as the code number 7-8-85 before I realized what I'd done. Rose's birthday, the number we'd always used as PINs for our debit cards, our garage, our voicemail access number. I hit *cancel*, and then didn't know what to punch in instead. The only other date I could think of was 11–17—November 2017, the month all this started.

EMAIL FROM AIYANA:

> I saw the date and realized it was the start of softball season over there. I miss those games. I wish I could be out there with you. I'd be your designated runner. Is someone doing that for you?

I rubbed the muscle under my eye preemptively.

> I don't want anyone to *do* things for me. I'm not looking for almost-sport, where we can all pretend I'm still just the same. I'm not the same. What's the fucking point of softball if someone runs for you? It's like eating carob while everyone else is eating chocolate but pretending you think carob's just as good, when everyone knows it's fucking vile. Also, it's too hot out in the sun for someone with MS.

The sun no longer slanted into the living room; I opened the blinds and saw Josh ambling up the driveway with a basket. He knocked. I limped to the door. He stood, basket at his feet, looking perplexed. He had never stopped by before.

"Haven't seen you about much," he said. "And Apple said you were looking not exactly."

Not exactly. One way of saying I had a disease that was trying to kill me and was surrounded by people who did not care one way or the other. "You should come in," I said. I was too tired to stand.

"Sure."

We sat in the kitchen. He put the basket on the table. "Got more than we need this year."

Neat rows of brightly colored squash, tomatoes, and peppers. And in the middle a carefully wrapped box like a double deck of cards.

"That's, uh. Weed's good for most things. I thought, y'know . . ."

I lifted it out. Unfolded the intricately creased paper—Apple's work, like the precise rows of produce. Inside was a plastic bag of five dried flowers and a small hinged metal box with an odd not-quite-lightning symbol on the lid. I opened it. A battery charger, two batteries, something the size of a big black pillbox labeled "Zeus," an oblong wooden-and-glass box with the same odd symbol, a tiny brush, and a short glass tube. I had no idea what it was but it seemed a miracle of compact engineering.

"That's just a loan. To see if vaping works for you. No rush to return it. We have two."

Of course they did. "Are there . . . instructions?" Instructions even a paranoid cripple could understand?

"There's YouTube videos. Or I could show you?"

A genuine choice. How novel. I nodded.

He pinched off a minuscule bit of the flower bud, opened the pillbox, which turned out to be a grinder, zussed the weed, slid open the glass lid on the vaporizer—it opened upward, like a folding razor—tapped in the weed granules, used the brush to center them in the trench, and inserted the glass tube. He did it fast and without thinking, as with any action set deep in muscle memory. He took one of the batteries and moved the black plastic cap from one end to another and slid it into place. "It won't engage until you press it in."

Engage what?

"So, here." He held it out.

I just looked at it, looked at him. "Show me."

"Sure." He resettled the box in his hand so the tube was toward him, and his thumb against the battery. "You push here. Wait six seconds." Lifted the box, and sucked on the tube like it was a breathing straw. Slow and steady. After a bit he waggled his eyebrows at me and let go of the battery, drew for another second or two, then lifted it away and breathed out. No smoke to speak of, but I could definitely smell it. He smiled dreamily. "We went with a heavy indica for you, but next time we can go lighter." He put the box gently on the table. "Want to try?"

"Later," I said. "Work to do first." I hated learning in public.

He could have grinned knowingly but he just said, "Sure," and stood. He no longer looked hesitant or uncertain. All those times I thought he was stoned he was probably just unnerved by reality. This was his real sphere of competence. "Just try it at the end of your day, y'know?"

I limped with him to the door. Opened it. "Josh? I—thank you. And thank Apple."

"Sure. Anytime."

Back at the table I pondered the thought that had gone into the whole basket. Rose and I had made fun of him for years in private, but he wasn't stupid; we always know how people really feel about us. Yet he had done this.

THE FIRST TIME I USED THE WEED—or, as I learned from You-Tube, took a hit with my Magic Flight Launch Box—I understood Josh's dreamy look. I sat spread like a star-fish on the sofa and felt no urge to do anything but stare at the ceiling for a week. It turned out to be twenty-five minutes. I slept without dreams. I woke up thinking, What would happen if I had an intruder while I was incapacitated? The next night I did not use it; my sleep was disjointed and jumbled. So I began to use a tiny amount at night just before bed. But during the day my anxiety levels kept climbing.

A week after Doug's murder I went numb from the hips down. I started on the IV prednisolone again. The nurse at the infusion center took four tries to find a vein in my left arm and get the cannula firmly seated. The weed was the only thing that helped me sleep. And being asleep was the only time I wasn't angry.

I was invited to speak at the Tempe, Arizona, meeting of the National Disability Coalition. Liang told me it was not a good idea. Rose told me I should listen to my doctor. "You're sick. You need rest. You need to stop and think and listen to what's really going on inside you instead of running around the country denying there's anything wrong."

"I am *not* in denial!" I shouted, really angry now. "This *isn't* about anger or hiding from fear. This conference is *important*. You think cripples should stay in bed and keep quiet and shut up, but I won't." And besides, they were offering five thousand dollars, and my health insurance was running out in six months. Five thousand dollars might just tip the revenue scale. I went, the cannula carefully bandaged for the journey. I left the weed, just in case this time TSA was paying attention.

Even in the terminal the Arizona air was so arid it seemed to lift my skin in its hurry to suck me dry. On the first day of the conference my right leg was useless and my left started to drag. I had to use a power chair for all three days. This time I expected to be ignored, so it hurt less. And this time I saw all those like me on the periphery: people in chairs, people with dogs, people with interpreters. But I was too tired to manage anything but the conference minimum, too tired to sort the new shape of the world or what it might mean. And I wasn't ready, not yet.

My insurance was good for now; a nurse came to the hotel every evening to give me an infusion. My arm swelled. I felt feverish. My fingers tingled and I couldn't sleep. My urine turned a strange color.

Important, I told myself. *Important. Nothing to do with fear.*

On the plane home, I collapsed.

It was like drifting through twilight. Cabin attendants with strong perfume. Being carried into first class. Stretchered off the plane on the runway. Bumpy ride in an ambulance. Voices: questions, questions. A monster reaching for me. An old woman's laughter like a creaking gibbet. *Just give up, lay down, and die.* Then nothing.

I woke in the middle of the night. A nurse was wiping my face.

"Hey, there," she said. She finished wiping my eyes. Deliciously cool. "Are you thirsty?"

I nodded. She helped me with some water. It was too dark to see her face. She adjusted something above my head. A drip into my right arm. "Wrong arm," I said, or thought I said, because the next thing I knew the room was monochrome with dawn and Rose sat reading her tablet.

"That old woman," I said.

Her eyes glimmered in the gray uplight like jewels in the face of an ancient god.

When I woke again, the room was hot with afternoon sunshine. My left arm was heavily bandaged. Rose was reading the paper this time. The headline was about the brutal rape and stabbing of a thirteen-year-old girl. *They came for that young girl. They came for Doug. They came because they could.* Rose wore shorts. Her thighs were close enough to touch. I knew exactly how the skin would feel.

I cleared my throat. "How did you get here? I mean, how did you know I was here?"

She folded the paper carefully, deliberately. Then she looked at me. "I'm still listed as your next of kin." In the daylight her eyes were as blank as marble.

Now I felt anxious. She might get up and leave me in this place. "Are you angry? Is it because you had to take time off work?"

"No. That is, yes. I mean—I just . . ." She lifted her hands, dropped them, seemed to be searching for something neutral to say. She plumped, in the end, for something practical. "It's Sunday."

I didn't understand that at all.

"The weekend," she said. "I didn't have to take time off work."

"Sunday." That didn't make sense. "Sunday?"

"You've been here three days," she said. "We've all been worried." She leaned over and smoothed my hair back from my forehead. Her hand was warm and soft. Unthinkingly, I pushed up against her palm, the way I had done since I was eighteen. She didn't take her hand away. I felt pathetically grateful. "I emailed Aiyana but didn't get a response. Maybe she doesn't use that email anymore?" When I didn't say anything she left it, and stroked my hair. "I've kept Christopher up to date. Josh is watering your herbs—I didn't know you grew herbs—and Granny Smith next door—"

"Apple."

"—is feeding Rip. I even called your mother in London."

The strokes were rhythmic, relaxing.

"You notice she didn't come rushing to your side." My mother. She had never liked Rose; the feeling was mutual. "I told her I was looking after you. I didn't think you'd want her. I promised to call again later today."

"Thank you." I meant it. The last thing I needed was my mother, fussing and taking it all personally: *God, what has our family done to deserve this?* as though it were *her* that was sick, *her* that sometimes couldn't even lift a tablet to read. "What happened to me?"

"Your adrenal glands stopped working. You have some kind of kidney infection. And the vein in your left arm collapsed."

So that's why the IV was in the other arm.

"Apparently, whatever they were infusing you with in Arizona wasn't prednisolone. A miscommunication in the order. It's the abrupt steroid withdrawal that caused the adrenal failure. And whatever they *were* giving you—some kind of chemotherapy drug and barbiturate, the ER doctor said—stripped out your veins. The kidney problems were because of that drug, too." She nodded at my shock. "You could have died."

You could have died. That wasn't supposed to happen, not from multiple sclerosis. Stripped veins. Adrenal gland. Kidney problems. All from a miscommunication. *It's aiming to kill you.*

———

THEY LET ME OUT after two more days. For my last day of prednisolone I bypassed the infusion center and drove to my internist instead. I trusted my internist. He specialized in HIV. His patients called Roy, his nurse, the vein whisperer.

I had to wait half an hour in the general waiting room. A young woman with narrow hips, arm in a sling, and a jawline slightly swollen under expert makeup sat in the corner looking defiant and defeated at the same time. My cane, the light bandage over the cannula, and the heavy bandage on the other arm reassured her; she relaxed a bit. I crossed one ankle over the other in the least threatening pose I knew.

She saw me looking at her arm and her chin went up.

"I hope you killed him," I said. "Or her."

"Fucker grabbed my wrist."

If I didn't have a cannula in one arm and heavy bandages on the other, I could have shown her two ways to break a wrist grab without even standing up. Before I'd figured out how to broach the topic, Roy stuck his head through the door. "Mara," he said. "You're up."

It was a bright room with warm prints, but as soon as he tore open the surgical wipe and the room filled with the scent of alcohol, none of the warmth mattered. The world narrowed down to my arm, the plastic embedded in it, the liquids they would soon force inside the swollen vein.

Roy wiped the cannula valve down, then inserted a syringe into the lock and started to push the saline. I winced.

"Bad?"

I nodded, afraid to speak. Superstitious behavior. If I didn't speak, I wouldn't really be here. This would not really be happening.

He pushed some more. I hissed. And this was only saline, to rinse the line through. The first of three lots of liquid. He slid the needle out of the lock, touched my vein gently. "The vein's leaking. We'll have to reinsert somewhere else."

I went away inside my head, then. Taking out an IV was just as vile as putting one in. More alcohol smells. Numbing sprays. Cold wipes. Pain.

No. No pain. I'm not here. It doesn't hurt.

Relaxation, that was the key. One PWA I'd counseled could not take opiates, and he told me once about a pain therapist he swore by. It was all about relaxation, he said. Deep breaths. Open those veins. The Tecfidera nerve pain had scattered my mind to the winds and made it impossible to try.

It did not make any difference. Should have got stoned, but then I'd never have got here. More pain. More. Was this what Doug had felt? I swore, and the room snapped back into focus.

"Damn, Mara, I know that vein's there somewhere. You're being so brave. If you can just stand for one more try, I'm sure we'll get it."

Why was it always "we" when they were hurting you? "No," I said.

"Excuse me?"

"No. I can't do this." I was getting tired of saying that.

"But—"

"No."

"I'll have to get the doctor."

The ultimate threat: Doctor will be disappointed. "So get him."

The doctor listened to me, looked at my veins, and frowned.

"I will not do this anymore. It's been more than a week. Do you know what it's like? I hate needles. I've always hated needles. I hate anyone touching my veins. If I even get a bruise on the inside of my leg or arm near a vein, I nearly faint. It's . . . Do you have any phobias?"

They must have drilled into them at medical school to never share anything personal. Remain aloof, impartial, untouched by human concerns. I kept my eyes fixed on his. He capitulated. "Spiders. The ones big enough to have knees."

I nodded at the bio waste bin inside which the bloody cannula dripped like a fanged predator. "Having that thing in my arm, *inside* me, inside my vein, for days, having to worry about it slipping, breaking me open— yes, I know it's designed not to do that, but this stuff isn't rational. Asking me for another IV is like asking you to open your mouth to let me drop in a tarantula." He swallowed convulsively. "I can't do it anymore."

He turned, a little pale, to Roy. "Would you get some ice?" Back to me. "I want you to lie down for a while. I'm going to make a phone call."

He left the room. His office was next door. Roy helped me lie down. I started to shake. He wrapped my arms in bandages and icy gel packs in alternate layers. I swallowed and swallowed, trying not to throw up.

Roy wrapped me in a blanket. "It's a bit of a shock reaction. Just rest." He cocked his head. "He sounds angry."

"The doctor?"

I must have sounded anxious. He patted my hand. "Not at you. At your neurologist. You shouldn't have been on this so long."

The wall muffled the phone conversation, but it got louder, then stopped. A minute later, the internist came back in. He was slightly flushed, and bright with that adrenaline glow people get after a successful argument. He started tapping out a prescription.

"I'm going to taper you orally on prednisone for a few weeks."

He said something else but my throat was bobbing and squeezing with relief. No more needles.

Hello? Hello, are you there?

JUNE. Hotter. The roar of the air-conditioning woke me in the middle of the night and often I didn't bother trying to get back to sleep. My dreams were full of shadows reaching for my throat, and now the weed just seemed to make them worse, so when it ran out I didn't ask Josh for more. After one particularly evil dream I woke up having difficulty swallowing. The yellow night-light in the bathroom showed what might be faint bruises around my throat.

Even though I was tapering, the second week on prednisone was worse than the first in terms of restlessness. I became easily irritated. I spent my time on Twitter, talking, sometimes arguing.

It was one of those nights, at four in the morning, that I heard about the robbery.

< . . . smashed up everything> said @SapphoCrip. <Weirdest thing was, after I'd cleaned up, I went into

the refrigerator to get the Avonex & found every single vial smashed and put back in the carton . . . >

<Weird> responded @SteveOTexas.

I didn't respond. I was clicking through to @Sappho-Crip's profile. A link to Facebook: Lory Hutchins, in La Crosse.

Smashed and put back in the carton. It sounded like the kind of thing a torturer would do.

<When did this happen?> I asked.

<When I was away visiting my brother in Madison. So . . . ten days ago?>

A month after Doug, only @SapphoCrip had been lucky enough to be out of the house. I do not believe in coincidence; I believe in data. I pulled up the CAT and PAWS mailing lists, hoping I was being foolish, that the prednisone was making me paranoid. But there she was, on both: L. Hutchins, La Crosse.

The CAT mailing list: a perfect tool for separating out those who would not be able to defend themselves, and it had been my idea. I had painted targets on our foreheads.

La Crosse. Less than two hundred miles from Minneapolis. Two hundred miles southeast from Doug's house. Two hundred miles closer to Atlanta.

AT NINE THE NEXT MORNING, shying at shadows, and jumping when Rip's name tag clinked against her bowl, I called the police. Captain Hernandez would not take my call. I asked his assistant to tell him I was reporting a potential hate crime. She passed me to a detective called Michaels who sounded bored and not at all interested in Doug, or Lory, or my mailing lists. "Yes," he said, "um-hm. I'll make a note." And I knew that as soon as I put the phone down he would wad up his note and toss it in the trash.

I tried the chief's personal number, left a message.

I called the Minnesota State Patrol and got transferred to their tip line staffed by a tired-sounding trooper. I explained about the mailing list, and Doug. "We'll look into that," she said.

"Please call me back and let me know."

"We have hundreds of leads to follow, ma'am."

"This one is important."

"I'm sure it is, ma'am."

I told her about Lory Hutchins, and the vials.

"I'll make a note of that."

It was exactly the same tone as Michaels's. "This is important. They both have MS. No one is paying attention—"

"And do you have MS, ma'am?"

"What's that got to do with it? Oh, I see. You think I'm a paranoid cripple. You think that just because I have

MS I'm not worth paying attention to. You think MS will kill me anyway so why bother."

"No, ma'am—"

"Well, fuck you and the patrol car you rode in on. Just *fuck* you!"

I called Christopher. "Stop selling the mailing lists."

"Just like that?"

"Yes. I'll explain later. Meanwhile, send me the contact info of every organization who has taken a list. As soon as you can, Christopher. Please." *Now*, I wanted to shout at him. *Do it now!* I could see a piece of paper, gray with burger grease, crumpled in the fist of a man as he scanned the names, planned their route . . .

The list materialized in Dropbox ten minutes later. Most of them were phone numbers only. I tucked in my earbuds and clicked on the first.

"My name is Mara Tagarelli. I'm on your mailing list. I want to be taken off."

"Your address, ma'am?" I told her. Faint ticking of computer keys. "Ma'am? I've removed it for you. If you're still getting mail after thirty days, please call. Thank you for calling and have a—"

"Wait. What do you mean, thirty days?"

"Ma'am, I've taken it out of the master list but there may be labels already in process."

"I want them stopped."

"I'm not sure—"

"I want them stopped. Not next week, or next month, but now. Today. If I get one piece of junk in my mailbox after next week, you'll be talking to my attorney."

"I don't have that authority."

"Then put me through to someone who does."

Dead air, followed by a few seconds of hold music. "This is Laetitia, floor supervisor. How can I help you?"

So I told Laetitia what I needed, again, and she explained that it might not be possible. I told her it better be possible or I would sue her and her company into the center of the sun. Before she could respond to that I told her I wanted an email address, too; that I would be sending a request for confirmation in writing of the action they had taken. Finally she allowed that, yes, she could do it, but her tone of voice let me know it was a terrible inconvenience.

I clicked off. Hundreds more like that to go. I took my lunchtime dose of prednisone, filled a glass with iced tea, and began. Halfway down the list my skin felt strange, hot and cold at the same time like a freezer burn. I could not keep still. I refilled the iced tea and started on the rest. Work, endless work. Climb up the bucket. Fall to the bottom. Climb again. Again, and again. I gritted my teeth.

Then they were done. I pulled out the earbuds. Checked my email. And then I couldn't put it off any longer.

I started a message to all CAT channels on Slack.

<ATTENTION: If you are on the PAWS list you are vulnerable. Be vigilant.>

Rip slapped through the cat flap. I reread the message. Not right. I erased it. Rip jumped up on the table. I picked her up and set her on the floor. She jumped up again.

"In a minute." I picked her up and dropped her on the floor.

She jumped up again and I bent her aside with one arm while I typed.

She patted my face. "Not now, Rip." I elbowed her off the table.

Still not right. I erased the message again. I should probably talk to the task force first. The mailing list had been a group decision, a joint recommendation to the membership. But it had been my idea. My fault.

<I think—>

Rip leapt up onto the keyboard. "Get the fuck *off*." I tossed her to the floor where she landed with a *thump*. Began again.

<I made a mistake. I think we all made a mistake.> *I'm sorry, I'm sorry.* <I think the mailing list is being used.> Rip leapt up once again, butted my arm, and when I did not pay attention, hooked her paw on the rim of the tea glass, pulled, and watched it fall, end over end, to smash in a shower of ice and glass.

I shot out of my chair, stood barefoot on a piece of ice, and bellowed. "Bastard!" Rip fled.

I hurled my chair at the wall. The photo of smiling, dewy me fell and broke. I kicked the table leg, then kicked it again, this time with hard focus. This was better than the punchbag. The punchbag did not crack and splinter and list to the side.

It was like watching a movie: someone else dropping their disguise as a civilized human being and defeating their governors. Someone else throwing, kicking, breaking. Jamming on shoes, throwing her stick in the car, grinning ferociously at her reflection in the rearview mirror. It felt good to be off leash. It felt free. I slammed into drive and roared out onto the road, texting with one hand and hauling the car around slow-poke vehicles with the other en route to the co-working space.

Some asshole without a blue placard had parked their Audi in the only crip parking space. I parked right against their driver's-side door so they wouldn't be able to open it.

Friday happy hour, sponsored by a wine distributor trying to break into the Atlanta market. Christopher said he would be there until seven. I pushed my way to the counter serving as a bar, grabbed a Merlot in a plastic cup and drank it in one swallow. "That's fucking nasty," I said to the woman who poured it, then picked up a cup of white wine and headed into the scrum. I used my stick to accidentally catch people on the Achilles tendon, where I knew it would hurt. "Sorry," I said, with that blithe cheer that meant I wasn't, and didn't give a shit who knew.

Christopher was sitting on the red sofa in the corner, holding court with two young men and a woman trying too hard to be one of the guys. When he said, "Mara!" they looked up at me with eyes like glazed fruit.

I leaned on my stick and swallowed down the white. Thin and so sweet I could not tell what variety it was meant to be. "Christ," I said.

Christopher just reached down, lifted a bottle tucked away by his feet, and raised his eyebrows. I held out the empty cup.

I fixed my gaze on one of the boy fruit. "I need to sit."

"Oh," he said.

"So either slide over or slide off somewhere else."

"Uh . . ."

"I'm not fucking kidding."

He stalked off, offended.

"You had to pick the pretty one," Christopher said.

"You'll find another."

"You can be such an ass," he said, but without heat. "So tell me about the mailing-list panic."

But the hum of humanity was what I needed, not work, not thinking about MS in me like corruption. "Just give me more wine."

The wine was crap but it was strong and it went down fast. It turned out that the man now fondling the knee of the woman also had a bottle. I noticed he poured more generously for her than anyone else, and that she was beginning to look a little glassy.

"You okay?" I said.

"Of course she is," her companion said.

"Was I talking to you?"

"M'okay," the woman said.

"You probably shouldn't drink any more. Do you know this man?"

"Oh, for fuck's sake," the man said. "Chris, who is this auntie?"

Christopher lifted his hands as though to say, *Hey, not my problem.*

And that was when the PA crackled to life. "A blue Jeep is blocking access to another member's vehicle. Will the driver of the blue Jeep move their vehicle immediately. They are blocking another guest's access."

Christopher looked at me.

"Now they know how it feels."

He closed his eyes. The man on the other sofa helped the woman to her feet.

"Hey," I said. And tried to stand up, but succeeded only in tipping myself half off the sofa. Huh. "Hey!"

A hand on my arm. Without thinking, I broke the grip and bent the hand back against its forearm.

"Aaaargh!!" Christopher, shaking out his wrist.

I struggled and stood, swaying. But the man was already steering the drunk woman through the crowd.

Would the driver of the blue Jeep—

". . . listen to me." He let go so abruptly I nearly fell over. "Mara. They're married. They're *married*. To each other."

—towed. Repeat, the driver of the blue Jeep should move it in the next five minutes or it will be towed.

"Also, that really hurt."

I was seeing double. I had never seen double before. Was this another MS thing?

—last chance. Last chance to move—

I swayed. The prednisone rage was ebbing. "Christopher . . ." I fumbled in my jacket pocket.

He sighed and held out his hand. I dropped the key fob in it and wove my way to the bathroom.

It was one of those with a code. I couldn't remember it, then I could remember it but it took three tries to get right. I had to squint. I did not understand how I'd got so drunk so fast.

There were three stalls. I lurched to the middle one—the middle one always had fewer germs, there were data—dropped my stick with a clatter, partly under the divider, and fell onto the seat with a sifting *thump*, like a sack of grain. I sat with my pants around my ankles, listing toward the wall, and shivered. The AC was set to Arctic.

I breathed. After a while it was easier to sit upright. Heat. That might explain it: I'd got too hot. Too much crap wine, too, maybe, but mainly hot.

After five minutes the cool air worked magic. Sitting up straight was easy, and I no longer saw double. I took several deep breaths. Another five minutes and I could text Christopher to meet me in the parking lot. No reason to face all those people.

A shadow fell at the bottom of my stall door, like someone peering to see if the stall was occupied. Then the door next to mine creaked. Great, an audience, just what I needed. Time to go.

A tap on the wall. Toilet paper, probably. I sighed, and began to roll up a wad I could hand under the flimsy divide between us. I wish people would check before—

A tap on the other wall. Adrenaline washed through me, as sickening and sudden as the warmth down your leg when your bladder lets go. Another tap, and another higher up, and another, and a shadow began to coalesce on the ceiling, where someone, or something, was creeping up the wall to the gap.

My shoulders turned to concrete. I could not move. *It's aiming to kill you.*

I needed my stick. But if I pulled it to me it would know I was here.

It already knows you're here . . .

I breathed, great gusts, in and out, in and out, and ran through the sequence in my head. Bend, grab the stick, pull it up and stand, pull up pants with one hand, open door, run.

I bent, pulled the stick—and it pulled back, so hard I nearly went over. I yanked with two hands, crashed back into the opposite wall, scrabbled at the door, and bolted. Silky laughter followed me as I burst into the main room, eyes staring, shirt hanging out and pants askew.

Outside, the night was warm, but I could not stop shivering. I sat on the step and texted Christopher.

I TURNED OFF THE LATE NEWS. Somewhere in the night I heard the faint whistle of a train. Car doors thunked down the street and people shouted goodbye; a neighbor's well-wined dinner guests were leaving. Not Josh; his guests would likely be stoned and peaceful, not drunk. I listened until I was sure they were gone, that there would be no stealthy steps up my path. Eventually I breathed more evenly. My legs ached but I didn't want to move; Rip had just curled up tight on my lap. The inside of her left ear was a swirl of creamy fur. Like cappuccino.

I stroked her, over and over, while she breathed under my hand. I had not talked to anyone all day. I had not left the house, even for the paper; it was still out on the sidewalk. This was how it felt to turn into a crazy old cat lady, the kind with six locks on the door and bones like sticks, the ones with the pinched faces who won't let anyone in the house, who call the police every time the guy from the gas company comes to read the meter. But they weren't crazy; they had good reason to be afraid. Old people were mugged and robbed and beaten all the time. They knew there were monsters. They were vulnerable. Like women, like children and small animals. Like cripples.

That morning the mail that plopped through my front door had included five pieces of junk mail. Three of them had the fake initial. I couldn't stop it now. *It's aiming to kill you. And I doubt you'll stop it.* Instead I had made it easier, offering names and addresses neatly listed. What would the oldest woman in the world with MS do? Set her pug on the crip-torturers and cackle while it savaged their ankles? But a fat, wheezy pug could not win against work boots, and a tire iron would make short work of her ruined raisin face.

I went to bed early, but like last night, and the night before, it took a while to get to sleep. And then I woke up thinking: Maybe it's not my list. I'd made assumptions about that man's intentions toward what turned out to be his wife. Maybe I was wrong about this, too.

I got up and began to dig through my spreadsheets, looking for commonalities. Age: Doug and Lory were both over fifty-five. Maybe they were on a list for older people? I couldn't think what. AARP? I made a note. Something to check later. Maybe they were on one of those terrible fake-peer-support pharma lists. I looked at their profiles, what meds they were on: Avonex and Aubagio. Different manufacturers. Not that, then. And maybe this was all coincidence. Two data points do not make a trend. I should be grateful to Rip for interrupting my message to Slack admitting liability. It might not be my fault.

But I still couldn't sleep. I got on Twitter. I sent a warning.

<Two of our members have been robbed. One was killed. Be extra vigilant.>

Nothing anyone could use against me; nothing actionable.

JULY. Day and night the air was like warm, sticky syrup. Off the prednisone, I felt hollow. Even with the modafinil I had no energy. I did not want to go back to the co-working space. I did not want to go to the dojo. I did not want to talk to Rose. Josh waved once or twice, and I knew now he noticed more than he seemed to. I'd got his number from Rose; in an emergency I could text, but I didn't want to talk to him. The only person I wanted to talk to was the oldest woman in the world with MS. I wanted to ask: How do you survive? How come you're still alive?

Barbra in Dubuque didn't respond to one of my DMs. She was as regular as clockwork: every night around nine, a bright little set of tweets about what inspiration she had gained that day and from what source. She was a flake who thought vaccines gave children autism and the government could control your mind. But she was our flake. She hadn't missed a day in months.

<Barbra. Please respond.>

Nothing.

. . . *the smell of cigarettes as he steps into the living room, rain shining in his hair. The list crackles in his pocket* . . .

<Barbra. I'm getting worried. Please respond.> My heart was beating too fast. It was too hot in here.

I got up, cranked up the air, and sat again at the laptop. I checked the PAWS list; she was on it. Not taking any meds I knew of.

Three data points did make a trend.

I used the landline—it felt more formal somehow—and got her number from information. As the phone rang and rang and rang, the places went through my head like a train-track rhythm: Minneapolis, La Crosse, Dubuque. Minneapolis, La Crosse, Dubuque.

My hand wrapped around the phone got colder and colder. Minneapolis, La Crosse, Dubuque . . .

I felt something on my shin and jerked back, half expecting the wheezing pug. But it was Miz Rip with her paws against my leg, mewing. I looked down at her and for one horrible moment I didn't know what she was. *Cat*, I thought. Then, *My cat*. Then, *How long have I been sitting here?* I was still holding the phone. I couldn't move my hand. The knuckles were white and the skin mottled purple and blue. *Death grip*. No, not yet.

The AC was roaring. I was half frozen.

Imagine you're getting into the bath. Imagine warm water rising up your legs, your hips, your waist. Relaxing your muscles. Now your back, elbows, shoulders, neck . . .

The phone fell on the rug. I could still hear the faint, endless ring on the other end. Rip sniffed it, then jumped when it started that awful shrilling howl. I turned it off and picked her up carefully, felt my hands warm. Carried her over to the thermostat, turned off the air.

I made myself coffee, very hot. While it cooled I called the chief's number again. Again I left a message. Paced. Looked at my phone. Nothing. Looked at the photo of the young me, back on the wall, now without glass. No glass meant no reflection; this way there was no chance of seeing anything that wasn't there. But without glass the young me looked naked and alone. On display with no protection. How had that old woman survived so long? What would she do in my position?

Minneapolis, Minnesota; La Crosse, Wisconsin; and Dubuque, Iowa. They had crossed state lines. I looked up the FBI contact info. No phone number, just an online tip form with a 3,000-character limit. I had to leave out things I thought were important.

After a bit of digging I found the phone number of the local field office and phoned. Straight to voicemail. I began a long, detailed message that was cut off after ninety seconds.

I imagined the old woman getting ornery. Maybe that's what it took. I could do that. I called back. And again, but it was hard to stay coherent in such small bits. The coffee was beginning to work. I thought for a bit, then wrote the whole story in 250-word chunks, complete with an introduction with my name and contact info, the subject matter—Hate Crime Murders Across State Lines—and the fact that I would be leaving multiple messages, each numbered and in order. I timed them, rewrote some bits. Then I called eleven times, and read, enunciating clearly, until I had given them every last detail.

It might be a waste of time. Most probably they would not even call back. I knew how it would go if they did. *A grown woman left her own house? And you expect us to do what, exactly, ma'am?*

Nothing. They would do nothing, because no one ever did. They just watched, glad it wasn't them. And often they could not see the thing that pursued us. Perhaps they did not believe it existed. But I had to try. Because I was the one who had laid the trail for the monsters.

I needed to talk to a human being, feel their breath, the vibration of their voice. The presence of others kept the monster at bay. I texted Christopher. No response. I called. He let it roll to voicemail.

I called the chief again. I told her I needed to report a hate crime but no one would take my calls, that I'd keep calling, every hour every day, until she responded. If I didn't hear from her in twelve hours I'd go to the media—if the media would still talk to me. Last time I'd sent a press release I'd had one tiny squib in the *AJC* Tuesday community roundup, in the same paragraph as the record-breaking sales of Girl Scout cookies by the Dunwoody troop.

My phone chimed: a text. *Hey, Mara. Not going around chain of command on this one. Go through Hernandez.*

That's who I was now: the cripple to be brushed off, of no more account than a twelve-year-old selling cookies.

I called the AMSS. It took two hot transfers and a call back before I even got the number for Wendy the counselor. It took her a moment to remember me. "Mara, right. You came to us once but never came back."

"Do you remember the old woman with the wig, and the dog?"

"The older woman? Of course—Junie. Junie's a pistol. She's been here longer than I have, longer than any of us. But she doesn't have a dog."

"It's a pug. With a yellow collar."

"No—"

"It wheezes, gets in people's purses."

"I'm sorry, Mara. Maybe you're thinking of some other group?"

"It was right there while the guy with—while Matt was talking about his numbness."

"I remember that. But you're mistaken. The DeKalb Community Center does not allow pets except registered support animals."

So that explained why no one took notice of the dog: it was against the rules. "Maybe you could give me her email address. Or phone number."

"We don't give out contact information."

"Does she, does Junie still go to the group sessions?"

"I can't give you that information, either."

"I won't tell about the dog."

"There's nothing to tell."

She was very good. If I hadn't seen it with my own eyes I would have believed her. "No, of course not. But just this once—"

"Ms. Tagarelli." Her voice was sharp. She softened it immediately. "Mara. I don't want you to get the wrong impression. So let me be very clear: in my group sessions there are not and never have been any dogs."

The dog was there. It wasn't a hallucination. The old woman had talked about it. But no one else could see it. I did not understand. How could something be real and not real?

I looked at the wall, touched the new table, my cold coffee mug. They were real, weren't they?

ROSE AND I HAD LUNCH at Murphy's while the ceiling fans turned overhead and tanned bodies in tight cutoff tees showing taut bellies moved past the tables, and bright, white-toothed laughter rang through the room. I felt very distant. Disconnected. Minneapolis, La Crosse, Dubuque. That was real, wasn't it?

"How's Aiyana?"

She thinks I'm paranoid and my life is an urban legend, if she still thinks of me at all. "I don't know." I turned over the spoons so I could not see anything reflected in them. But when I picked up my water glass a face leered at me from behind my left shoulder and I banged it down hard enough to slop.

"Mara, I'm worried about you."

I mopped at the mess with my napkin.

"You haven't eaten any of your lunch."

I picked up a piece of bread obediently.

"And you're using two canes, now. You look terrible."

Minneapolis, La Crosse, Dubuque. They were coming for me.

"Christopher says you haven't been in all week. Mara? Mara!"

"What?"

"What's *wrong* with you? You're like a zombie. And what's with the spoons? You're getting sicker, you haven't been in to work, and now you act as though I'm not here." She leaned toward me. Her eyes were very bright. "It's my birthday today, have you forgotten?"

I stared at her blankly. Birthday. What do birthdays have to do with being stalked? But she didn't know it was coming for me, it was already in me, turning me into a doily brain, eating me from the inside.

And then the brightness in her eyes overflowed and dripped down her cheek. I reached out, touched the tear. It was warm. "Don't cry."

"I'm worried about you." She wiped the tear away with the heel of her hand. "I read your cards." Perhaps she wanted me to ask what they said. But I didn't believe in them. And even if I did, I didn't want to know. "What's happening with you?"

I think I'm losing my mind. I think MS is eating my brain. I think I'm being hunted. Or haunted. But I don't believe any of that. Belief is not data. It's not real.

She put her wet hand on my wrist. Anchored me.

I tried. "You were cross because I wasn't facing my fear. But it's not . . . I can't . . . How can I face something that's stalking me?" Playing with me. "That's coming."

"What? Who's coming?"

It. But I could not tell her about that. Like the dog, it was real and not real. "The men who killed Doug." They were real. And I'd written them a personal invitation.

She poured hot water in a cup, added a tea bag. "Here, drink this. But keep talking."

"Doug was killed in Minneapolis."

"That horrible torture case in May? The guy with MS?"

I nodded and sipped at the tea. It burned my mouth but I didn't want to pick up the water glass again to get ice. "He was on my mailing lists. And then a woman in La Crosse—a woman with MS, on my mailing lists— was robbed."

"Your mailing lists?"

"It's all my fault."

"It's not your fault. You didn't attack them. It's no one's fault but the attackers'. Isn't that what you used to say? Anything else is blaming the victim."

I could not disagree. But it was still my fault.

"Was she hurt? The woman in La Crosse."

"She wasn't there. But all her Avonex was carefully smashed and put back in the carton. It was the same men."

"They did that at Doug's house?"

"No," I said impatiently. Couldn't she see?

"But then how do you know it was them?"

"It just was. I know."

"Drink some more of your tea, Madame Zara."

"It's too hot. But it was them. I know it was. There's something . . . calculated in what they do. Sadistic."

"They're probably just meth heads who have fried their brains." She pulled my tea over to her side of the table and added a little milk.

"And now I think they've got someone else. A woman who lives in Dubuque. She's tedious, but she shouldn't have had to die like that."

She pushed the tea back to me. "It was on the news?"

"No." I sipped at it. It was better with milk.

"Did someone call you?"

Nobody calls me anymore. "She didn't reply to my message."

"She didn't reply to your—And you think that means she's lying in pieces around her backyard?"

I didn't say anything.

"Okay, Madame Zara. Did you call the police?"

"I called the FBI."

"The—okay. And what did they say?"

"Nothing. They won't say anything. They're like everyone else. They think I'm a paranoid cripple."

She was looking at me the same way she used to when I ranted on about men and their violence and how they beat and raped us because they could. "Maybe this one will be a false alarm, too."

IT WASN'T. It was on my news feed. This time they burned all the evidence, including Barbra. The fire was so severe that six other apartments had gone up, and the whole complex had been evacuated. I called Rose first. She did not pick up. "Watch MSNBC," I told her voicemail. "The apartment complex in Dubuque. They got her." *It's aiming to kill you.* And I had laid it a trail.

Then I called the police and told them I was coming in.

Michaels turned out to be younger than I'd expected from his tired voice. He was sipping coffee at his desk, surrounded by stacks of files flagged with Post-it notes. I limped over. He stood up long enough to clear off a chair. He was tall, rangy. The hand he waved for me to sit was big and dark-knuckled. "I can spare five minutes. We had a double homicide this morning." His clothes were rumpled but he was freshly shaved. I wondered if he kept a razor in his desk. "You say you've got some evidence this time." He didn't talk to me in that sympathetic, reasonable tone people use with cripples and children. Perhaps when you'd learned even a nine-year-old could shoot you, you never took anything for granted.

"Another woman on my mailing list was murdered."

He sipped at his coffee.

"And it's the same people."

"What's your evidence?"

"How much evidence do you need? Two murders, one break-in. All on my list. All in a straight line."

"A straight line to you?"

"It's not just about me."

"How many people on your list?"

"It's not coincidence."

"How many?"

"About twenty-eight thousand." More than a thousand joined just last month, mostly via Facebook. More this month, too, but I hadn't looked at the totals.

"So say one murder per fifteen thousand." He rubbed his jaw. "The murder rate in the U.S. last year was four-point-nine per hundred thousand. That works out at . . ."

One per 20,408.

". . . well, not much different. Could be coincidence. Could be another list. What evidence do you have? Because a theory isn't evidence." He sounded like me that first time with Liang. *Belief is not data.* Something must have shown on my face. "Ma'am, as I've explained before, it's outside our jurisdiction."

"I called the FBI."

"Well, they're probably the right people."

"I told them everything. I told them they're coming this way." Even to me it sounded crazy. But it wasn't. I knew it wasn't.

"Coming for you?"

Anger swelled in my gullet like a fist. "How tall are you, six-two? About one ninety? And you carry a gun at all times. And a badge. When was the last time you woke up in bed afraid? When was the last time you saw a TV news report about a six-foot-two man with a gun being raped and sodomized in a park by a gang of six teenage girls while he was out jogging, and then thought, 'That could have been me'? Lately? No. Because you don't see images online, in books, on TV of people like you being *got at*, over and over. Look at me. *Look* at me! I used to be able to run ten miles and benchpress you. Now it's hard to open my own front door."

He was sipping at his coffee, tired, not really listening. I leaned forward.

"How many men have you arrested that would like to see you dead?"

"I don't—"

"How many!"

"A few." He shrugged. "A lot."

"Then imagine this: you've been shot in the neck. Modern medical science breathes for you, but you're completely paralyzed. Someone parks you in your wheelchair in the middle of the prison yard in Fulton. All the guards walk away. Imagine the eyes on you, the crippled cop. They know you're helpless. They know that they can do anything to you and get away with it. They smile. They discuss it among themselves loud enough for you to hear. One takes out a shank. Another grabs his crotch suggestively. They start walking toward you. Coming for you. Imagine the sweat on your upper lip. The fear. They know they can get you."

He was watching me now. He had no idea. That fear, that *waiting* for something to happen was like being buried alive. As the weight of the earth on your chest piles up you can't move, you can't breathe, and then the dirt starts hitting your face.

"I got through the fear the first time. Made myself, *forced* myself to see I could fight back, that I wasn't helpless, even though everyone, everything, told me I was. But now I'm going through it all again, because now I *am* helpless. Now I can't even run away." I was wound up tight, motionless. Now all I could do was wait for them to come.

He looked at me with enormous compassion. But compassion was not evidence.

———

THE LAST TIME I had been this angry, this afraid, I trained my body to a blade. But now I had MS. I went to a gun show to avoid the waiting period and got a Ruger .38 SP101. A short-barreled revolver with a black rubber grip. I got two boxes of shells, a clip-on belt holster, and another holster to attach the gun to the side of my bed at night. Then I went to the range.

Women and men were created equal, one of my mom's vintage posters read, *and Smith & Wesson makes damn sure it stays that way*. But *Don't rely on a weapon*, my self-defense instructor had said. Easy for her. She was six feet tall and could punch through cinder block. Crips have fewer choices.

I slid the chubby, slick shells one by one into the cylinder and clicked it shut. Maybe this is how the oldest woman in the world with MS survived. Or maybe she was just crazy. Then I started shooting.

I WAS PUTTING DOWN RIP'S FOOD when my phone chimed. A text from Anton.

<Hey, Mara. I hope all's well. It would be great to catch you up on what we're up to here at GAP.>

I blocked his number. The next time I was at the range, every target was his head.

SEPTEMBER. Johnston disappeared off the net in Louisville. Two days later it was Carmella in Nashville. Kentucky State Police said they'd get to my inquiry in due course. Tennessee did not bother to hide their impatience. I phoned the FBI again and left another message: They're coming.

THEY'RE COMING. *They're coming.* It was the drumbeat of my days. I went to the range every afternoon. Every evening I slipped the Ruger into its leather holster and clipped it onto the end of the long flat board that went between the mattress and box spring. Every night I fell asleep with my hand touching the butt. The old woman cackled in my dreams.

THEY'RE COMING. My eyes flick open. The bedroom is hot and thick and silent. My heart lumps under my sternum, like a huge crank turning. *It shouldn't be hot.* Someone has turned off the air-conditioning.

The noise, when it comes, is tiny, like a mouse nosing at a piece of paper. From the dining room. My throat is as dry as a corpse's eyes.

They're coming.

My mind is slippery with panic and my muscles are blocks of wood. *Think. Think.*

Another noise. This time from the small hallway outside the bedroom door. Without taking my eyes off the door, I feel down the side of the bed for the Ruger.

The handle begins to turn. A soft laugh. The door opens. Light glints on something, a ring, a knife, as a hand emerges from the shadow, and I lift the gun, realize from the weight that it's not loaded, it's not loaded—

—and I woke up hunched against the headboard of the bed with my knees drawn under my chin and Rip staring at me from the comforter. The air conditioner droned steadily. It was not even midnight. Josh had left his light on again. The pillow next to mine was empty.

I pulled the Ruger from the holster and broke it open. Five rounds. But I turned on all the lights and, stick in one hand, gun in the other, went through the house room by room. All the doors were locked, all the windows secure. The light on the security system control pad blinked green. I turned it off, and then on again.

I got to the kitchen last, then had to sit. I was shaking all over. I stared at the picture of the still unformed me with Elton John. The healthy, vital teen who smiled exultantly back was an utter stranger to me.

Why do you think they're coming for you? Michaels had asked. Because they were *always* coming. Because they could. And now they were in my dreams, making me do this to myself, saving themselves the work.

ROSE LOADED MY SUITCASES into the Subaru, while in the house I pushed a reluctant Rip into her carry cage. She mewled unhappily. "It's just for a few days," I told her. She scrunched down in one corner and wouldn't look at me. *Please, don't make this any harder.*

"I'm taking the week off work," Rose said as she drove us north, to the suburbs.

"Thanks. I'm glad Louise doesn't mind." Rose was concentrating too hard on the road, checking her rearview mirror too often, all to avoid meeting my gaze. Oh, no. Rose taking a week off work. "Rose, were you and Louise planning a—I mean, I don't want . . ." Barging in, upsetting their lives. I stared fiercely out the window. "Shit."

"I want you with us. Louise is just going to have to do what I want for a change."

So they had argued. I watched her driving for a while. From this sideways view her irises were thin slips of green gel. I wondered how long it would be before she allowed herself to understand what I already knew: she and Louise were not going to last.

ROSE CARRIED MY CASES into a bedroom with twin beds in front of big casement windows that overlooked a tidy, suburban garden with a swept lawn and rose bushes that she had not yet had time to subdue.

"Hope you'll be comfortable," she said. "Take a few minutes to settle in."

I closed the door and opened Miz Rip's cage. She was backed up in the corner. Her fur was matted, as though she had slept in alleys and eaten from garbage cans for a month. I felt like a monster. "Come on, little one." She wouldn't come out. I sighed, and filled a bowl with crunchies. "Come on, Rip. Crunchies." She meeped pitifully. "I know you don't want to be here. I don't much want to be here, either. And I'm sure Louise doesn't want either of us. But here is where we are, just for a little while." *Until what? Until my life was miraculously restored to me?*

I hung my belt with the Ruger over the bedpost, and unpacked.

IT WAS A LOVELY HOUSE. Cool in the afternoon when the October sun warmed the garden to seventy-five degrees; warm in the evening when the temperature fell to the fifties. It was still humid in the mornings but by mid-afternoon you could feel the air drying itself out for winter. I made sure I got up late enough in the morning that Louise had already left for work. She worked late every night I was there—and I made sure I went to bed before she got home.

By the second day, Rip was out of her cage, but too scared to leave the bedroom. She would mewl mournfully by the door and I'd open it, but when she saw the strange hallways instead of the familiar wooden floors she ran under the bed.

"I'm worried about her," I said to Rose out in the garden later that day. "She's not eating enough."

Rose was weeding; I was supposed to be reading but I couldn't concentrate. The words kept rearranging themselves into lists of names, and the dry leaves that blew this way and that across the lawn rustled like sinister laughter.

"She'll get over it." Grit of fork in dirt as she rooted around a particularly stubborn weed. "How's Aiyana?"

"She doesn't talk to me anymore. Nobody wants a cripple."

She winced, just as straight people used to wince when I called myself *queer.* "Maybe it's not that."

"It is."

"It must be so different for her out there. And you've been so angry. I know how that is." She saw the look on my face. "I'm not excusing her. But are you sure? Maybe you've got the wrong—"

"Two different email addresses. Skype. Voicemail and text. I'm sure."

"I'm sorry." Rose dug some more, pulled the weed. Took some time shaking the dirt free of the roots. "But it's not her I'm worried about."

"I'm fine," I said automatically. But I wasn't. I woke in the mornings with my whole body tight with listening. If someone were to tap my skin with a fingertip, it would boom like a drum. "It's Rip *I'm* worried about."

"Maybe you should try bringing her out into the garden with us."

Cats bond with places, not people. "I should have left her at home where she feels safe." *Where she feels safe.* Where would I ever feel safe? Where did those women in the slings feel safe?

An unexpected shower sent us indoors, not summer rain hard enough to beat flowers to death, but gentle, almost benign. Rose made chamomile tea. We sat and watched the water runnel down the windows. My shoulder muscles were as hard as ball bearings.

"You were always thinking ahead," Rose said as though picking up a conversation. "I thought that was crazy. The moment, that's what I thought was important: the right-here, the right-now. But I find myself living a life I don't understand, that I'm not even sure I like, and I don't really know how I got here. I've been thinking: maybe you were right to think ahead, to make all those lists, to plan. But it terrifies me, deciding ahead of time how things should go. And I realized that it must be terrifying for you the other way around. You're used to planning but now you can't because you never know what's going to happen from day to day." Her eyes were gray green in the rainlight, and candid. The tea steamed when she lifted it. "You said to me the other day you were trying to face your fear. So, have you?"

My knuckles were white around the mug handle, my thigh muscles clenched under the table. I hadn't been able to eat a full meal since that dream. Was being scared to death of what may or may not be real the same as facing my fear?

"No," I croaked.

She just nodded. "Nor have I. I don't know how. I've been reading my cards but I'm not sure I believe them anymore. Maybe they really are just bits of pretty colored cardboard."

"I must have been a pain to live with."

"Sometimes." But she smiled. We could have been talking about two other people.

"Don't give them up," I said. "If they help, don't stop."

She shook her head, not in disagreement, but the way people do when they discover something they thought was worthless was valued for a small fortune and are afraid to believe it. "So now I'm the one who thinks they're just pretty pictures and you're the one with premonitions and hunches? Life is very strange."

"Yes." Rain spangled the window, turning the afternoon into an abstract painting. "Do you want to hear something really strange?" She nodded—what else could she do?—so I told her about the MS support group. Wendy the terrible counselor, the helplessness in the room, and Junie. Her claim to be the oldest woman in the world with MS, her diagnostic visions, and the pug. "Only no one else could see it. At least that's what Junie thought." I did not tell her Wendy's behavior matched Junie's belief. "And there was a woman with a broken arm. One at the internist, too. In a sling. And Junie threatened me."

"She broke a woman's arm?"

"What? No, not that kind of threat."

She looked as though she had questions but she did not ask them.

"She told me a grinning monster was coming to kill me. And that I wouldn't stop it." I swirled my golden tea and realized that in Rose's house I was not afraid of seeing anything that should not be there; for two days I had seen no menacing shadows, no reflections of distorted faces, had not felt something ravenous flitting from corner to corner when I was not looking. That made no sense. "I think she meant MS." Hers was a wheezing little pug and mine a monster. But they weren't real. But if they weren't real, how come we had both seen the dog?

"Malevolent old bat."

I nodded.

She reached across the table and took my hand. "Well, fuck her."

"She should be so lucky."

Our smiles were as comfortable as old clothes. But worn thin. Soon to be set aside. I squeezed her hand and let go.

"Keep reading your cards," I said. "Read them for me. Read them now." One last thing we could share. "Please."

They were new, at least to me: big cards, made of thick linen board with an opulent blue-purple design on the back. She laid out six, facedown, in a cross pattern on the table, then another four in a line to the left.

"This is the Crowley deck," she said. "They're based on Egyptian designs, because Crowley believed that's where the cards came from originally. Your first card." She turned it over. "The Priestess." A bare-breasted woman with a crown and sun disc. Fine hatching of lines and whorls to represent power. "I think it's based on the goddess Isis. Anyway, this represents where you are now."

Isis, protector of the dead.

"This second card is more about your current sphere of influence."

The words didn't mean much but the rhythm of her reading was hypnotic and the cards themselves were rich jewel colors. I sipped my tea, rolled the yellow taste over my tongue, watched Rose's supple fingers turning the cards, tapping them for emphasis, tracing the designs. The first six cards of the cross were all faceup now.

Rose paused, hand on the next card. "This card, the seventh, is the key to the whole reading. This card tells you about your attitude, about what is influencing how you feel and what will happen in the future. I think of it as the perspective card." She turned it over.

Big Roman numeral. XIII. A bearded man wearing the crown of Upper Egypt, wrapped like a mummy.

"This is interesting. Osiris. King and judge of the dead."

"Death," I said.

"Not exactly. It more often signifies sudden change. Unexpected change. It can mean loss, too, but it's more about transformation. It's a very strong metaphor. Death as metamorphosis. Which is true, if you think about it."

Not really. Dead is dead.

"I mean, nothing really ends or is destroyed, it just changes form. Like a snake shedding its skin."

Having MS did not make me a different person, it did not make me better or special, just a person with impairments. Physically less. Where does the light go when you switch it off? It's gone.

"See those things in his hands—the crook and flail? They're symbols of Osiris's power over death. He's not just the dying god, he's the dying and rising god. Death as a leaving behind, a shedding, or rebirth. Painful, and terrifying, like all births, but not fatal, not final. Change, not death."

I did not believe in rebirth. Death was final. And it was coming. Doug and Barbra had already met it. Yet something inside me shifted and settled, snicked into place. I picked up the card with its bandaged god—cocooned, metamorphosing—and stared at it.

"Do you want me to read the others?"

"Yes," I said. "Fine."

The rest of the day was eerie and quiet. I felt enclosed in a bubble of silence. I don't remember eating that night. I do remember that I slept well and without dreams.

Rose woke me up at eight in the morning. Her face was pink and strained, like a red rubber band stretched to breaking point.

"What's wrong?"

"You'd better come and watch the feed."

Jim Parnetta in Chattanooga had been found cut to pieces with his own butcher knives.

THIS TIME Detective Michaels called me.

I was shown into an interview room. I leaned my sticks against the wall. Michaels introduced me to the woman with him, a detective from Chattanooga. The Minnesota police had finally sent out a BOLO, and Michaels had seen it that morning and connected the dots. He called the Chattanooga Police Department.

I told them everything I knew. Again. They asked me questions. I answered them. Everything was still coated in that eerie crystal of unreality. I was still scared, I would be a fool not to be, but I was no longer paralyzed, unmade by it. Some decision I had made was rising to the surface, though still hidden.

Michaels was pleased I wasn't at home and suggested I stay at Rose's, "for the duration."

"No," I said. "Every time there's a serial rapist out there, police say: 'Ladies, stay indoors for your own good!' Why don't they ever say: 'Men, don't rape. Men, there's a curfew; inside by ten or we'll cut off your balls.' Why should I stay away from my home? Why should I let these people terrorize me into lying down and turning my face to the wall?"

And that's exactly what I had been doing. Giving up, giving in, turning away. *It's aiming to kill you. And I doubt you'll stop it.*

BACK AT ROSE'S HOUSE the autumn afternoon was round and rich with sunlight. Autumn, the season of change.

When I said I was going back to my house, she didn't protest. We held each other for a long time. She smelled of the leaves she had been burning in the garden, of the dirt preparing to take in acorns and pine cones and cradle them in the dark over winter while they waited for spring, their time of rebirth.

"Here," she said. "This is for you. I hope it helps." Big Roman numeral. The king of dying and rising, staring up at me from his cocoon.

THE FIRST THING I DID when I got home—before I even took off my coat—was open a packet of cat food for Miz Rip. She was gobbling from the plate before I had even finished squeezing it out. I shrugged. Let her eat from the table this once; there might not be a tomorrow. I leaned on my stick and rubbed behind her ears. She spared me a quick purr.

On the wall in front of me a healthy young woman stood next to Elton John and beamed exultantly at the world, at her future. I had no idea what lay in my future now. I lifted the picture down, unclipped the frame, and slid the photo out from the mat. The death card was in my pocket. I slid that between the mat and the backing instead, and hung the picture back on the wall. It would do for now.

A knock on the door. But when I opened it I found only a basket of winter squash.

THE AMSS RAN YOGA CLASSES at a storefront studio on McLendon called Whole Life Yoga. It was a few blocks south of the Flying Biscuit, just east of the entrance to Candler Park, where I had met Aiyana and played softball. I'd never noticed it before, but I'd never been a yoga kind of person. Then again, I'd never been a victim, never been a cripple, never looked ahead and seen empty space. Things change.

There were nine people. The instructor at the head of the room was not a young, lithe Athleta-wearing blonde but about forty; plump, pleasant, and welcoming. Seven women and one man faced each other along each side on mats. That is, six women sat on mats and one in a power chair. Another chair was parked by the door; a manual chair with power-assist hubs blinking in standby mode, and WHEELED FREEDOM stenciled around the tires. I kept looking at it.

I did not realize I'd been expecting Junie and her pug to be there until I saw she wasn't. The instructor, Helen, pointed me to the shelf of yoga mats and then nodded at the pale fifty-year-old blinking behind her glasses and said, "Sit next to Mary." A clipboard went round for names and contact info. I gave email address, phone, and Twitter. Helen promised to send the list out to everyone by the end of the day. Then she asked us to introduce ourselves, for my benefit I assumed, as they all seemed to know each other.

"Drew," said the tall man. "Diagnosed last year. Relapsing-remitting. Just moved with my wife, Rosami, from Philly. I was getting my JD. I got my JD. Not that I'll use it now." He had that jerky, random look I was beginning to associate with brain lesions. For a moment I imagined I saw a sheet of flame flickering over his head.

"Rosami," said the woman next to him. "Not MS but Lyme disease."

We went down the line: RRMS, SPMS, PPMS, RRMS. The woman in the power chair had very precise diction, a number 4 brush cut, and spinal degeneration. For the first time I introduced myself as "Mara, RRMS, diagnosed last year." Mara, RRMS. I wondered if I'd live long enough to say that again.

After the intros, Helen looked at us one by one and said, "What do you need?"

"Balance," Drew said. Helen nodded.

"I've been dizzy," Mary said. "And I keep forgetting things. Like yesterday—was it yesterday? Maybe it was the day before. I was saying to John, well I was trying to say to John, you know how he is. He's my husband," she said to me.

"Dizziness and memory," Helen said before Mary's word cataract flowed again. Mary seemed more relieved than upset at being shut down. "What else?"

"Shoulder. As usual," the woman in the power chair said.

A neck, a tingling foot, more balance, fatigue. When no one had anything more to offer, Helen said, "We'll start on our backs," and everyone except the woman in the power chair lay flat.

Helen tinged a bell.

"Think of your breath as the tide," she said. "It flows in and out, washes up and then back down, at different speeds and different strengths. Every beach is different and every body is different. Just breathe naturally, feel your lungs fill and empty, let your muscles soften and connect to the earth . . ."

The earth was a bamboo floor over poured concrete, but martial arts instructors talked about grounding while we stood suspended over the ground on mats

on top of sprung wood floors. I was used to the metaphors. And the rhythm of breath was an old and easy
habit. In, in through the nose, out, out through the
mouth. In and out.

Then we started with simple arm movements, reaching up and up, one side then the other, stretching. From
there we went to easy poses: child's pose, cat-cow, and
then what I'm pretty sure weren't yoga poses but simple
hamstring stretches. We worked on necks, shoulders, legs,
feet. Each stretch or pose flowed into the next and felt
good.

We ended flat on our backs again. The fancy chair
had switched to sleep mode.

"Now think of your breath as a square," Helen said.
"Equal on four sides. When I begin, breathe in for
the count of three. Hold for the count of three. Out for the
count of three. Hold for the count of three. And with
me. In two three, hold two three. Out two three, hold
two three."

Once the room was breathing steadily she went to
four, then five, then six. Our breath lengthened, the
square stretched until that's all there was in the world.
Up one side, across the top, down the other side, along
the bottom. A cycle. A fine cycle, with others in the same
rhythm. I felt good in a way I hadn't experienced since
that night when I reached for the milk and fell down. A
whole room full of people breathing together, peaceful

and relaxed. Perfectly blank but for the square and the breath. And then Mary, the doily brain next to me, started to snore. No one laughed. She was one of us. We just breathed on.

If they didn't get me first, I'd be back.

I WALKED HOME SLOWLY up McLendon, enjoying the not-quite warm afternoon. The sun was very bright, shining unimpeded through bare branches. Far away someone was burning leaves.

My phone rang. GAP. After a moment I answered it.

"Mara," Anton said. "How are you?"

"I'm well." I could be dead tomorrow, but today I'm well.

"That's good to hear. Very good." I did not ask him how he was. "Listen. I'm glad your break has done you good. I was hoping you might be willing to help us out with a couple of things."

My break. I kept walking, watching a squirrel running along a phone wire.

"Mara? Hello?"

"I'm here."

"Are you willing to come in and talk to us?"

I nodded at a woman with a stroller. "What did you have in mind?"

"Well, as I say, we could use your help with a couple of things."

"In what capacity?"

"Consulting."

The squirrel was gone. "New ED not working out?"

"Let's just say we might have been hasty."

"So." I lifted my face to the sun; it might be the last time. "You're willing to pay an outrageous consulting fee to someone with, as you put it, emotional lability."

"Outrageous is not what—"

"My hourly rate is one seventy-five, including travel time. Plus expenses."

"We're a nonprofit! We can't—"

"I'm the one with lesions on the brain, but you seem to be the one forgetting. I wrote the budget, Anton. I know exactly what you can and can't afford. That's my rate. Three-hour minimum. Let me know." I thumbed out of the call and set the phone on airplane mode.

LATER THAT EVENING I sat at my laptop. I had loose ends.

> I don't know why you won't talk to me. Maybe it was a mistake to change our friendship. I don't think so, but I don't know. Maybe you just don't know what to say about me having MS, maybe it freaks you out.

I'm adjusting—No, I'm figuring out I have adjustments
to make. There's a lot. A lot of shit to figure out. And
maybe we're going down different paths now. Maybe
it's for the best.

The reply came back, bang, before I could close the
email window.

What the fuck? No!!! It's not the MS that freaks me
out, it's your bitterness. It's hard to talk to an angry
person.

And it's like what happened between us doesn't
exist. You never talk about us. How am I meant to
process that?

Every email: just you and your shit. I get that it's
big. I really do. But did you never think I might have
stuff? A new job in another country—another
country where they all sound weird and the racism is
different and the light switches are upside down and
they drive on the wrong side of the road. I *want* to
talk to you. I want to talk about *us.* I want you to
listen. Can you do that?

I touched the screen with my fingertip. Breathed in a
square until I felt calm again.

I don't know.

I breathed around the clench in my belly, the visceral memory of her toes curling, her soft skin under my mine.

I'm different now. If I'm still here tomorrow—

Different, yes. I thought I had faced my fear, but instead I had pushed it below the surface. It's hard to think when nine-tenths of your mind hangs frozen and inaccessible, hard for friends to approach when what remains glints in the sun leaving those who come close blinded.

I deleted what I'd just written.

I'd like to try. Tomorrow? Let's Skype.

I sent, waited one minute, two, ten, then closed the lid.

I prepared for bed slowly, almost ritually, folding clothes into perfect lines, canceling airplane mode, and placing my phone in the exact center of the bedside table.

Doug had not had a neighborhood watch. Lory had not had an alarm system. Jim had no gun, or neighbors. They had not been ready. I was. More than ready. I slid the revolver out of its holster. The rubber grip was warm and snug in my hand. I rested the barrel along my forearm, squinted down the sights at the door. The trigger fit my finger nicely.

If they walked through the door now I would smile at them: *This is a Ruger*, I would say. *It will change your life.* And I would squeeze, and the jacketed bullets would punch neat round holes in forehead, throat, stomach. Not change for them. Just pain, and death, real death, and rotting in their winding-sheets. And I'd be safe. I swung out the cylinder—five full chambers—and snapped it back into the frame. I might have MS but I was not a helpless victim. I put the Ruger away, thumped my pillow, and reached to turn off the light.

The phone rang. Atlanta PD. I picked it up cautiously. "Yes?"

"Ms. Tagarelli? Michaels. We've got them."

For a moment I had no idea what he was talking about. *Got them.* "I'm sorry, I don't—"

"They were in a bar. In Dunwoody. Drunk. Trying to sell off the stuff they got from Parnetta's place—"

Got them.

"—list on one of them."

"Wait. They did have a list?"

"Yes, ma'am. Hold on. Something called Monster. They had . . ."

He kept talking but I was not listening. Monster. *MonSter!* Beating heart of the MS community. Their subscription list. Their list, not mine.

". . . of them circled."

"My name was on it?" Of course it was. I was a subscriber. "Was it circled?"

"Lots of names were circled, yes. Including yours. But you're safe now. Free to go about your life."

Silence. "You're sure?"

"They'll be in jail for the rest of their lives. Which won't be very long if they're tried in this state."

, "Thank you," I said, dazed. "Thank you very much." And put the phone back in the precise center of the table.

Safe now. I turned off the light. Lay on my back. Stared at the dark. Safe. Free to begin again on my own terms. To do better. Free to find out who Mara RRMS was.

That's when I heard the whisper:

You'll never be free.

"What?" I sat up. But there was no one there and the house was silent.

You'll never be free of me.

It came from the living room. Rip wasn't on the bed. The Ruger had disappeared.

Just you and me and you'll never be free.

Outside the door. A low laugh.

You and me.

The whisper hissed like dead leaves against the door. There was no other sound. I couldn't hear my own heartbeat, my breathing. The door began to open outward, the wrong way, and from the shadow crept a hand, a wrist, a forearm. A shoulder. Glimmer of pale ribs. *And I doubt you'll stop it.*

I closed my eyes. "No . . ."

Yes. And the whisper was in my room. *It* was in my room.

I opened my eyes and looked.

Hello, it said.

It was naked and lean and strong, and it was me. It smiled, wide, wider, like a pat of butter melting in a skillet, and it had too many teeth.

I ran. It ran too, silently, smoothly; that was the worst part. We ran and ran until the walls whirled about us, as though we were on a carousel, and then the carousel stopped, just stopped, and we were in the kitchen, and everything was still except for *it* walking toward me, laughing silently.

Closer, closer, and all I could see was the flat muscle sliding under the skin of its arms and the picture on the wall behind its right shoulder.

It's aiming to kill you. And I doubt you'll stop it.

My monster grinned at me. And flexed.

I jumped like a rabbit.

Then, "No," I said. "No. You *want* me to run." It wanted me to hide, to be afraid. "No, you want me to be ashamed."

It's not me. It's MS.

"I see you," I said. "I know what you are."

And I did. This was not MS. This was helplessness and self-loathing and second-class citizenship. It was the story of what it was to be a cripple in the world: relying on the kindness of strangers. Smiling hard at the stairs and hoping for a miracle—having to hope, because there was no ramp. Feeling seen only as a target. Seeing yourself as a target because that's how others saw you.

Break the narrative.

I leapt at it.

There was a soft whole shock, as though I had thrown myself full into a taut sheet of plastic film. I wrapped my arms around it and stood toe-to-toe, belly-to-belly. Skin-to-skin.

"Fuck you," I said. "I. Am. Not. Less." And I squeezed, squeezed until its skin pushed through mine, until its face was against mine. "I exist. And I will fight." I squeezed until cartilage passed through cartilage and bone fused with bone. "If you're close enough to hurt me I'm close enough to hurt you. So fuck you." I squeezed until I had both hands on its backbone, and the backbone pressed up against my stomach. I felt like a boa constrictor swallowing, swallowing, and I squeezed more, until it had no breath in its body, until it *had* no body, squeezed until I woke up, hugging myself in my kitchen, arms around ribs, laughing, crying, myself.

I am not invincible. But I am not Less. I refuse that

story. I'll fight it; I'll teach others to fight it. Teach self-defense, too. I'll teach from a wheelchair if I have to. I'll even teach the oldest woman in the world with MS, and she'll teach me—she already has. So fuck the story of Less, and fuck MS. Ha, no. They should be so lucky.

ACKNOWLEDGMENTS

No one—not even me—knew I was going to write this book. You are reading it now only because everyone involved in its publication was able to get over their initial surprise at its existence and swing into action with the kind of speed and precision only possible with a real team. I am delighted and amazed that they cared enough to make it happen so fast.

So thank you, Stephanie Cabot, my agent; Sean McDonald, my editor; Steven Pfau, my publicist; Jeff Seroy and his whole team; Maya Binyam and Sara Birmingham, Abby Kagan and Logan Hill, Rodrigo Corral and Boyang Xia, and everyone else at FSG.

Most of all, though, I want to thank all those people over the years who have helped me overcome my occasional emotional gracelessness in the face of growing physical impairment. I've had a lot of help from the disability community. I particularly wish to thank Riva Lehrer and Alice Wong, whose intelligence, compassion, and generosity have been guiding lights. Special thanks also to Kenny Fries, Susan Nussbaum, and Joanne Woiak. There are scores, perhaps hundreds, of others whose simple presence has been invaluable. Many know who they are but some might be surprised to find out how much what they said or did mattered.

ACKNOWLEDGMENTS

Thanks, too, to Chris and "Helen," who donated good money to excellent causes and trusted me with their names.

Finally, thank you to friends and family—and they definitely know who they are!—especially, always, to Kelley, who I will marry as many times as necessary.